The Boutique

Open

I mmerse yourself into the lives of nine extraordinary people, and discover more about their equally extraordinary lives. The thread that connects them is The Boutique. And their resilience.

What people are saying

The Boutique, some words from an award-winning author.

"This book of short stories took me out of my usual sphere of reading material and into a world closer to real life and the lives of authentic characters.

The stories are short but are never wanting – characters are well-rounded and genuine, situations are not 'roses around the cottage, chocolate-box' perfection, they are gritty, real and poignant. I connected with every single one of Ms Blick's people and understood each setting and storyline.

Ms Blick is one of those naturally gifted storytellers that a reader would feel privileged to have found.

I will be looking for the next book from this author. I hope I won't have to wait too long."

D M Gent
Author of Ash and The Favour Man
Frederick Forsyth, People's Book Fiction Prize winner 2024

with love

Dee Blick

About the Author

Dee has been a creative writer and avid storyteller from just eight years old. Her fascination with words, woven into stories continued at secondary school. Influenced by the careers' advisor telling her she should write stories for a living, she embarked on a career in marketing. She has spent the last 41 years merrily creating copy for her clients. During this time, Dee has also enjoyed training people in the art of producing compelling and engaging content, winning several awards for her work along the way. She then turned to authoring books. Dee really found her feet with her second book which became an international best-seller, leading to a publishing deal in China. Global publisher, Wiley, produced her third book and in the last few years she has picked up a couple of reader awards for two of her books.

When it comes to putting pen to paper, creative writing and storytelling remain Dee's first love. She now has more time on her hands to write without interruption and so has penned her first fiction book, The Boutique. Will there be a sequel? It depends on what readers say!

Born in Leeds, in the North of England, Dee lives in West Sussex with her husband, a mere stone's throw from her two married sons. She has a gorgeous little grandson who visits grandma and granddad every Friday and enjoys indulging her youngest son's French bulldog Psmith (with a silent P). He sleeps over every Wednesday.

Dee loves talking to aspiring authors, encouraging them from the sidelines and on occasion rolling up her sleeves and acting as an author mentor.

࿆

Dee's photo was taken by the super talented Sophie Ward

Foreword

The Boutique was born out of a conversation with Josh, who styles women for a living. I was chatting about my long-standing idea for a book, a collection of short stories, with a slimming club as the central hub connecting the personalities. Josh suggested a fashion shop, instead.

I was hooked, given the catwalk calls to me far more than weekly weigh-ins. I suspect I'm not alone in this matter. For years I had thought about writing a book based on likeable, often complex individuals, each with their own compelling story to share. With my fictional fashion shop, The Boutique, I could now take readers on their journey, with this glamorous boudoir, the starting point.

So, when you initially tune into a chapter you may be joining a light-hearted conversation about clothes or, the dialogue will pique your interest because there's something more sinister or complicated afoot. I wanted to merge the light with the dark and in doing so build story-lines that were gripping, with the final twist in every tale, unpredictable.

My first task, however, was to work on the nine personalities. The advice given to me from Eve Richings, a journalist and writer I respect, was at the front of my mind: 'make sure you create characters that your readers care about.' This resonated with me because when we're rooting for someone we become invested in their story don't we? We form a close connection, and we want them to succeed.

So, I took my inspiration from many of the special folk that have touched my life over more years than I care to remember. I then added my vivid imagination into the mix and spent several months creating these nine people. During this time, I really got to know them. Finally, I was happy to introduce them to their world.

Friends asked why I wanted to write about hard hitting themes such as abusive relationships, homophobia, bullying, compulsive behaviour, and addiction. For many of us, our lives have been affected to a greater or lesser degree by one, or more of these. And for me, fiction works well when intertwined with facts. If the author gets the balance right with real-life subjects, the narrative can be intriguing and dare I say, uplifting.

I hope you find each one of these special humans relatable and inspiring and when you've left one, you can't wait to meet the next.

So, please get in touch and tell me what you think about The Boutique and who you identify with.
You can find me on Facebook and Instagram.
Dee X

Dedication

In memory of my beautiful friend,
Michelle,
whose courage, laughter
and kindness
never dimmed.

The Boutique

Nine captivating short stories
Where fact and fiction merge

❧

Dee Blick

This book is proudly published by Dee Blick

Powered by
Filament Publishing Ltd
14, Croydon Road, Beddington,
Croydon, Surrey CR0 4PA
www.filamentpublishing.com

The Boutique by Dee Blick
ISBN 978-1-915465-71-9
© 2025 Dee Blick

❧

Table of Contents

If they don't like you
for being yourself,
be yourself even more.

Taylor Swift

Chapter 1

Jake

Jake was no fan of Mondays. Customers at The Boutique were usually thin on the ground and many of those that did pop in were in browse mode only. Monday was the busiest day of the week for refunding those customers who had bought in haste and repented at leisure over the weekend. But today, Jake was relieved that it was Monday, grateful to be going to work. The weekend had been an emotional roller-coaster.

He was glad to see the back of it.

Jake lived with his mum who had dementia. The disease was progressing at an alarming rate. This weekend, two innocuous events - losing her purse and misplacing the back door keys - had sparked outbreaks of hysteria. He arrived home on Saturday afternoon to find his mum sobbing uncontrollably, telling Jake that she wished she were dead. After hours of searching and trying to placate his mum, her purse had turned up in the washing machine, the keys in the oven, slowly baking.

By Sunday night, he was mentally exhausted, resentful of the fact that his sister was nowhere to be seen on these now frequent occasions. Looking after his mum had fallen at his feet. Thankfully, there was enough money in her pension for her to attend a specialist day care facility. Nevertheless, at the age of 30, he felt that he was too young to be her de facto carer.

Passing the barber shop window, Jake caught sight of his reflection. Looking good!

The reflection had changed dramatically in the last 10 years, thanks to Jake losing a significant amount of weight, and in the process, reinventing himself with an effortless sense of style. This was in no small part due to the design scholarship he had been awarded at college. His skills at sewing and design, plus the intuitive ability to style women of all ages and body shapes, had marked him out as an exceptional student. The 12-month intern-ship, in Paris, was with a fashion house that regularly graced the covers of Vogue. Being awarded the scholarship was something quite special. But, after a year of conforming to a rigid hierarchy, and of being surrounded by people that were more invested in what they looked like than in honing their talent, he decided to move back to England.

Within a few weeks of looking for work, Kelly offered him the job of managing her shop, The Boutique, and he jumped at the opportunity. He loved the job of styling women and indulging his passion for fashion.

Appraising his fresh and preppy look in the barber's window, a thought crossed his mind. In seconds he was taken back to a dark time, his last year at school. Being gay as well as overweight had made him a target for the boys in his tutor group. It started with them hurling verbal insults, but progressed rapidly to throwing objects, especially in classes where the bullies were guaranteed encouragement from a packed house. Anything that came to hand was used as a missile: lunch boxes, books, half eaten pieces of fruit and more. Much of it arriving when he was least expecting it. He tried to brush off the humiliating and sometimes painful incidents and would do anything he could to look as though it didn't bother him.

Some weeks the bullying was so overwhelming that it was a huge relief just to make it to the weekend without falling apart. In the safety and comfort of his bedroom, he could immerse himself in his hobby, styling and sewing, which gave respite from physical attacks and insults for 48 hours at least.

His parents were oblivious to the torment their son was going through. He did not want to confide in them, and his sister was far too absorbed in her own life to see what was happening to her brother. As for the teachers, Jake suspected they were aware of it, and they did nothing about it.

He was on his own.

Jake's walk to and from school had become increasingly torturous. The bullies followed him or laid in ambush, eager to bestow some punishment for daring to be gay, daring to be overweight.

For daring to be himself.

He had reached the point of no longer wanting to live, when salvation emerged in the form of Christine and Michelle, twins that had joined his tutor group a few weeks previously. The twins were accepted immediately. They were attractive, outspoken and funny girls who loved sport and fashion. They saw what was happening to Jake and took him under their wing. They were not afraid to call out the bullies' behaviour as it happened, ridiculing them openly, forcing them to experience first-hand what it was like to be the unwanted focus of derision.

And the twins were not in the habit of backing down.

They were fearless, loud and persistent. Their 'twinness' was undoubtedly their Superpower, and they put it to best use when defending Jake. The abuse ended within weeks, including the attacks that Jake had experienced on the way into and home from school.

It was a friendship that continued to blossom long after school and college. Christine and Michelle visited Jake in Paris and they still made a point of catching up with him every few weeks. Jake would be forever grateful to them for standing up to the bullies at a time when he needed it most. They saved him when he could not save himself.

In the years after leaving school, Jake had often thought about the boys that had bullied him, in particular the ringleader, Simon Watson. He egged on the others and used his size and sporting prowess to inflict misery upon Jake. He might not have always been at the front of the queue to throw the first punch or hurl the first projectile, but he made sure that Jake's life was a misery for the entire school year. Until Christine and Michelle entered the frame. Thankfully, that chapter of Jake's life was far behind him, and now he was popular and celebrated for who he was. Customers loved him and consequently, he often found himself being invited out to dinner, the theatre, even hen parties!

His social life could be filled to the brim if he accepted every event to which he was invited. With a vulnerable mother to look after, however, he had to ration his social life so that wherever he went, he was always close to home.

Jake was now a man in demand and he loved it!

Walking briskly to work, Jake's mind turned to the jobs for the day. Quiet times were good opportunities to promote The Boutique, especially to their 100,000 followers on Instagram. Jake had become a hit on social media with his sharp wit and his on-point styling tips. Monday was the day designated to run a live online style-session and to create content promoting a selection of clothing and accessories in The Boutique.

He was looking forward to it.

"Jake! I've been waiting for ages. I thought you opened at 10 o'clock. I want to return the dress I bought on Saturday and I'm not happy with the bag you sold me last week. It's just not right."

Jake's heart sank. This was not a good start to his day. Prepare for battle. He knew what was coming.

"Morning Steph. We don't open for 15 minutes, so

if you want to grab yourself a coffee and pop back at 10.30, I'll be ready and waiting for you."

Steph was a serial returner and she really knew how to get Jake in a fluster.

Out of every three things she bought at The Boutique he could guarantee she would return two of them. Always in the same bag, pristine, wrapped in the original tissue paper, often unopened. And for the items she did keep, there was always a drama. The dress was not as well made as she originally thought, so could she have a discount? The sunglasses were a bit too heavy on the bridge of her nose, so could she swap them for another pair? She had seen a similar item in another shop, cheaper, so could she have a credit note for the difference? And on it went.

Her reasons for returning items, and her dissatisfaction with the things she kept, at times bordered on the ludicrous.

Serving Steph put Jake's customer service skills and patience to the test virtually every time she visited The Boutique, her accompanying bag filled with the clothes and accessories she had bought just days before. The only time he had refused to issue a refund was when she'd tried to return a pair of trainers four weeks after the 14-day return period. She started crying, which then escalated to shouting and screaming at him. The Boutique's returns policy was unfair, she claimed, and she demanded her money back. Jake stood his ground. He eventually issued a credit note which she begrudgingly accepted. A few days later, she returned to apologise with a box of chocolates and some flowers. She was forgiven, but the whole drama was not forgotten.

And now here she was again.

Jake was going to have to start his day by refunding her for the dress, and then listening patiently to her reasons for returning the bag; the very same one she had fallen head over heels in love with a few days earlier.

After the weekend with his mum, he could do without this as his first transaction of the day.

"Can't I just wait inside, Jake? I've just had a coffee. I won't disturb you; I promise, and I'm so cold from waiting for you to open."

She used the voice of a little child, a tactic she was prone to adopt when negotiations were impending. Her bottom lip puckered, and she shrugged her shoulders with an over dramatic shiver. She held out the bag for him to take, which he dutifully accepted.

"Erm okay, Steph, but I have several things to do before we open, so if you're happy to wait…"

His voice trailed off as he opened the door and let her inside.

"Thank you. I promise I'll be quiet."

Her little girl voice continued, but this time took on a jubilant tone. She had won the first stage of the battle.

With his opening tasks completed, Jake turned to Steph who adopted a different persona altogether. In place of the little girl was a woman with a look of grave concern. She waited for him to start the proceedings.

"So, Steph, what appears to be the problem?"

He almost added 'this time' but stopped himself before the words tumbled out of his mouth. Now was not the time for sarcasm. Steph was still a customer, albeit an extremely testing one. He just wanted to refund her for the dress and allay her concerns about the bag. He could have sold that many times over. Steph had got to it first, but only after asking him to walk her through every feature of it in excruciating detail.

He should have known the next twist in the story. History was not on his side. Steph went in for the kill.

"The bag...well, where do I start? Everything is wrong with it. I don't like the handles, Jake. They're so impractical, and the cross-body strap is too thin, it will hurt my shoulders. You know how I suffer with pain in my upper body from too much typing. I just won't get the wear out of it. And the colour. It's too... bright."

She let out a loud sigh and threw her hands up in the air. It was all very dramatic. And all very Steph.

"But Steph, looking at the tissue paper, you haven't even unwrapped the bag. When you were trying it out, we talked about the grab handles and how they were not supposed to be soft because of the structured style of the bag. And you did say that the crossbody strap was perfect for your shoulders..."

Jake's voice trailed off again. There was no point trying to put forward any case for the defence, no matter how watertight the evidence. Once Steph was in this frame of mind, the conversation was only going one way, and Jake was on the losing side of it.

"I know, I know, but I've had time to think about it.

I shouldn't have bought it. I don't like it. At all. It could damage my shoulders. I won't get the wear out of it. I'd like a refund. Here's my receipt."

She spoke in a loud, clipped and combative manner which was usually the precursor to a full-on rant.

Jake had heard enough. He didn't want to upset her. He knew it was game over.

Battle lost.

"That's no problem, Steph, please don't worry. I understand. Would you like a refund or a credit note?"

He already knew her answer.

"Refund to my card, pronto please, Jake, thank you."

Steph made a miraculous return to her smiling and pleasant former self. In place of thunder clouds and lightning was bright sunshine.

Mustering up a smile, despite wanting to scowl at her, and feeling irritated by her use of the word 'pronto', Jake processed Steph's refund. His day was going to start once she had left the shop. She was still hovering, but her attention had now turned to the jewellery.

How many times this year have I processed refunds for Steph? Must be at least 10, so I reckon I'm going through this whole rigmarole twice a month. If I owned this shop, I'd ban her. I don't know how much longer I can keep on smiling at her no matter what she throws at me. Everyone has their breaking point and I'm close to mine.

His thoughts were interrupted by the phone ringing.

"Hi, is that Jake Reid?"

"Yes, speaking. How can I help you?"

"What time are you open 'til today? I'm looking for a gift for a friend."

"Ahh, that's lovely. We're open until 5 o'clock today. Oh, and we can gift wrap any item at no extra cost."

"That's great. Thank you, bye."

Putting the phone down, Jake noticed that Steph was still looking at the jewellery. He silently prayed she would not buy anything. He couldn't face the futile exercise of more tissue wrapping, only for the items to be returned days later, untouched. Going by her recent purchasing patterns she was clearly on a run of returns.

His prayers were answered.

"Bye, Jake, and thank you."

"Goodbye, Steph. Enjoy the rest of your week."

For the rest of the morning, Jake kept himself surprisingly busy with customers. And happy days! Most were buying, not browsing. A few were Instagram followers that had seen his latest video promoting the new lines of knitwear and snazzy zodiac themed blouses. He always liked it when his online content translated to sales.

The till was ringing. His mood had changed for the better. The encounter with Steph was now firmly behind him, and he was already 50% up on last Monday's sales. Kelly would be very pleased with him.

Later that afternoon, just as he was about to unpack a large box of ankle boots, the door opened, and a nervous-looking man approached the till. Jake noticed that he looked unwell. His skin was pale and marked with what looked like scars from acne. He also seemed uneasy.

"Hello, how can I help you?"

"You're Jake Reid, aren't you?"

"Yes, that's right. Did you call earlier about buying a gift for your friend? I recognise your voice."

"I did but I wasn't telling the truth, sorry. I wanted to check that you worked here."

Jake was puzzled. What could this stranger want? And why would he lie about something so benign?

"And why is that, may I ask?"

Jake summoned his most assertive voice, meeting the man's gaze.

"You don't remember me, do you?"

"Can't say I do. Should I?"

"School. Sixth form...I'm Simon Watson."

Jake looked at the man, aghast. Simon Watson from the sixth form? The ringleader of the bullies who made his life a misery. The boy who excelled at sport transformed into this unhealthy-looking, pasty bloke standing in front of him? Really?

The man shuffled awkwardly, hands in pockets, avoiding Jake's gaze.

What on earth did he want?

Jake was not going to allow him the first punch. The floor was his now.

"Simon Watson...well how you've changed. I didn't realise it was you, but I do remember the bullying, and that you were the ringleader. Telling all your mates to throw things, and to hurl every homophobic insult under the sun at me. And how could I forget those journeys home? I seem to remember you egging your mates on to stuff soil down the back of my shirt. Oh, and to pour fizzy drinks over my head. And the times you threw my school bag into the river? And the fruit, the fruit, even during lesson time. How many times did I have to dodge an orange or a banana? I have vivid memories of the living hell I went through, thanks to you and your friends, Simon."

Pausing to gather his breath, Jake continued in the same vein. His heart pounded; he was on fire. Nothing was going to stop him now.

"And I'm sure it was you, Simon, who emptied all your lunch box leftovers into my backpack when I wasn't looking. I remember that you found it hilarious when I went to get my books, and your half-eaten rubbish fell out onto the floor. The teacher blamed me for it. And how you all laughed when I had to clear it up with just my hands and some tissue paper.

Yes, I remember it all, just like it was yesterday."

Jake could not believe the words that were coming out of his mouth. But oh, he had longed for this moment. He spoke in a calm and slightly menacing manner, articulating each word, occasionally pausing for effect, as if he were an actor delivering his lines to a hushed audience.

He was not going to fluff it now.

He could see the impact it was having on Simon, he stood rooted to the spot, occasionally glancing at Jake, but mostly just looking at the floor. Jake had finally found the voice that had been buried deep inside him for far too long.

But what on Earth did Simon want? Jake decided to stop talking, take a breath, and wait.

Eventually Simon spoke in a faltering voice.

"I know...I know it is awful. It's terrible what I did to you, Jake, just terrible. Appalling what we, sorry what I, put you through. I accept in full, everything that you've said. And that's why I'm here today... to say sorry to you, Jake. For the last year I've been working with a counsellor who's helping me with my addiction to prescription and street drugs. A big part of the work I must do to live a clean and honest life, is to make amends to the people that I harmed throughout my life. You were at the top of my list, Jake, because I know how much harm I caused you. I don't ask for your forgiveness. I have no right to ask for that, but I want you to know that what I did to you was, well there aren't the words to describe it. I don't know how you managed to keep it together and…

…I hope you can see that I make this apology to you sincerely, and from the bottom of my heart."

He finally looked at Jake, and whilst there was no doubting his sincerity, it was clear that he found the whole experience terribly awkward.

Although Jake listened carefully to every word that Simon said without interrupting, he was far from finished. He had more to say, and Simon was not going anywhere until he'd said it!

"I wouldn't say I 'kept it together', Simon. Far from it. I had to cope with what you and your mates inflicted on me because…"

He paused for a few seconds.

"…well, I hardly had a say in the matter, did I?

Do you remember asking me if I was a girl or a boy, every single day? And calling me a fat slob, or worse, because I didn't do PE. I spent every PE lesson holed up in the library because I knew what would happen if I put one foot inside those changing rooms. I can't tell you the number of mornings when the thought of standing in the middle of a busy road was more appealing than going to school. If it hadn't been for Christine and Michelle..."

Jake paused again. He could feel his emotions rising. But he wanted to hold himself in check so he could deliver his stream of consciousness to Simon without falling at the final hurdle.

"...I don't know if I would be standing here today. But I am, and I've made a good life for myself. As you can see, I'm not the frightened, overweight, insecure person that you and your friends tormented all those years ago. Far from it."

Jake stopped and looked at Simon, who, if his face was anything to go by, was consumed by remorse and shock. He clearly had not expected Jake's response to be so assertive and so detailed. This Jake was not the young and vulnerable boy he and his friends had bullied remorselessly.

A long silence followed. The atmosphere in The

Boutique crackled. Jake was relieved that it was just the two of them in the shop. He shuddered. How awkward would it be if a customer walked in now.

Eventually Simon spoke again, his voice breaking as he did so.

"I can never make complete amends for what I did to you, Jake, I know that. But I want you to know that I am so very sorry...I can't take back all the awful things I did, or what I encouraged the others to do. But...but if it's any...consolation..."

He stumbled and paused, searching for the right words.

"...if that's the right word...after I left school I had a bad motorbike accident. One thing led to another, and I ended up addicted to drugs. I lost everything. Job, home, girlfriend, self-respect, you name it, the lot. I'm now rebuilding my life, bit by bit, but it's not easy, and every day is a struggle. It is getting better though, and I can see that your life has turned out well. You deserve to be successful, and you look so well."

Sensing Simon on the verge of tears himself, Jake softened his tone. He had said enough to him. The point had been made, and vigorously so.

"Simon, I accept your apology. And thank you for having the courage to come here today, and for what you've said to me. It can't have been easy for you. It does mean something, but I had to tell you what it was like for me at school. I hope you can stay off the drugs and get your life back. And I do hope that life continues to improve for you. It's too precious to squander."

Simon smiled, letting out a huge sigh of relief.

"Thanks, Jake. I've said all I wanted to say, really. Thank you for being so...well thank you for listening to me, and for your kind words."

At that moment the phone rang, and when Jake looked around after answering it, The Boutique was empty again. He wasn't disappointed, though. That entire experience had felt surreal.

Thankfully, the shop remained empty for a few minutes longer, allowing Jake's heart rate to calm down a little. His head was still spinning, but he was no longer trembling. Never in his wildest dreams could he have anticipated something like that. He felt strangely exhilarated, and completely vindicated. But for now, he had to put all this to one side, get back into work mode and unpack it later, at home.

The phone rang again. Boy, did he hope that the drama was finished for the day.

"Hi Jake, it's Becky. I'm just checking that you're in today, because I'm on the hunt for jumpers. And those glorious jumpers you were showing in Sunday's Instagram video are right up my street. Also, there's a strong probability I'll pop into The Roasted Bean beforehand, so is it a caramel latte as usual?"

"I am most definitely in, Becky, and it will be lovely to see you, as always. And as you know, I never turn down a caramel latte. That is so kind of you. I'll see you soon and I'll put some of those jumpers to one side for you. I know the ones that will have caught your eye."

Becky was Jake's favourite customer. She was bringing his favourite coffee, too.

Wonderful.

Monday was shaping up to be a very good day after all.

Our greatest glory is
not in never falling,
but in rising every
time we fall.

Confucius

Chapter 2

Becky

Catching sight of Becky walking towards The Boutique always put Jake in a buoyant mood. She was a stylist's dream. She carried herself with confidence, having planned her outfit for the day to match her mood - invariably sunny. Coupled with this, she often arrived at the shop with his favourite coffee, a caramel latte, ready for a chat, and usually with a credit card waiting to be put to good use.

Today, Becky dressed head to toe in black and white. A vibrant pink handbag, and trainers with vivid pops of cobalt blue and neon pink completed the perfect ensemble. Becky was never one to blend in - one of the many things that Jake liked about her. She was adventurous with her fashion, she was funny, and she had a generous clothing allowance! If Becky liked an outfit, the chances were that she would buy it, along with any other items that complemented it. If she really fell in love with a jumper or a t-shirt, she would often buy them in several colours. Unlike the customers that spent time deliberating over a purchase, often returning several times before deciding whether to buy an item or not, Becky bought on instinct. She was not one to waste time. Jake aptly described her decision-making process as: 'I like that...let's try it...I love it...show me the other colours...I'll take them.'

This all added up to an enjoyable experience for them both. Jake could count on Becky to spend, and in return, Becky could rely on Jake's candour and experience as a stylist. He would never try to force a sale on Becky, preferring instead, to present the clothes he felt confident she would love. He then left it to her. If she asked for his advice he would give it, even if sometimes it was not what she wanted to hear. In those situations, Becky liked his diplomatic phrase: 'No, I'm not feeling it with this.' Similarly, if he really liked what she was wearing, his phrase: 'Absolute knockout!' was very well received.

Now here she was, wearing a big smile, balancing two large coffees precariously in one hand, her glamorous pink handbag nestled in the crook of her arm, the winter sun highlighting the golden tones in her chestnut brown hair.

"Well good morning, Becky! Aren't you just a vision of loveliness? What an outfit. I'm very much into the whole monochrome vibe with the candy pink. Are they new sunglasses, perchance? Chanel? Very stylish."

Jake stood back to admire Becky's outfit. She had nailed it again. He didn't mind that on some days, such as today, she wore an entire outfit purchased elsewhere. Becky had several shops in her little black book, but it was rare for a day to go by when she didn't wear something from The Boutique, even if it was just a piece of jewellery. She was a great ambassador for Jake and Kelly, featuring in many of their videos and photos. The Boutique was, without doubt, her favourite place to shop.

"Good morning, Jake! Thank you. I was hoping you would approve of today's ensemble. It's my fashion-steal outfit! The whole lot, including trainers and handbag came to less than £250. Excluding the sunglasses, of course. It's a supermarket-inspired shop. I love creating a designer vibe on a small budget."

She handed Jake his coffee.

"Now, please take this before I spill it on the floor, which is what nearly happened in The Roasted Bean. I collided with an open door! Yes, the sunglasses are new, and as you so correctly spotted, Chanel. They were an indulgence. I bought them in the airport last week, and I'm more than a little obsessed with them."

Jake laughed. Becky was notoriously clumsy, as well as generous with her coffees.

"They really suit your face and look so chic and luxurious. And you know my saying about style: 'I don't buy expensive; I just look it'. Chanel aside that is, of course. Thank you so very much for the coffee. After the morning I've had, a caramel latte is most welcome, I can tell you."

Jake decided not to divulge any details of his earlier encounter with Simon. He was still trying to process what had happened, so he put it to one side to discuss with her another day. He had grown close to Becky over the last few years. Love of fashion aside, they shared a gentle sense of humour, and both loved a good gossip. Today was not the day for diving deep and baring his soul. It was all about Becky, who was clearly on a mission to find a snazzy jumper, or more likely, several snazzy jumpers.

He pointed at the rail, freshly curated after her earlier phone call.

"I've put some of our new jumpers in your size on this rail. I'm certain they're the ones you were getting excited about. You saw the others when you came in on Saturday morning. See what you think."

Jake could see in seconds that his choices had hit the mark. Becky flicked through the rail, pulling out jumper after jumper, accompanied by her usual commentary.

"I like this one...adore this one...not for me by any stretch of the imagination, don't like the colour. This one is divine."

Within minutes, the rail stood empty, barring only a couple of jumpers, and she headed for the changing room with the running commentary continuing.

"I am just loving the multi-coloured jumper with the pink accents. And the one with the blue accents. Not keen on the red jumper with the lace sleeves. I like it but it doesn't like me. It clings too much to my middle. I'm now trying on the jumper with the faux fur cuffs. Oh my, this is the one. So much so, I think I'm going to take three of them...the black, the silver grey and this fabulous honeycomb colour. They all look great with my hair, which is a big plus. It's a big no to the winter white. It's much too pale for my liking and...

...I've worked hard this month, Jake, and packed the hours in, so the clothing allowance is a bit bigger than usual."

Jake laughed. It was Becky's usual way, fast and furious.

She had lost weight in the last year, and embraced her new figure, 'making up for lost time' as she described her updated style. Gone were the days of hiding beneath baggy clothing. She was now open to trying on clothes that skimmed her figure. Feeling trim and confident, she had donated most of her old clothes to a local charity shop so she could free up room in her wardrobe for her new outfits.

"Right, Jake, prepare for lift off!"

Within ten minutes of entering the changing room, Becky had tried on everything and emerged, triumphant, her arms full of jumpers.

"I've left the ones I don't like in there, and I'd like to go with these, please."

She handed him six jumpers.

Jake was not in the least bit surprised by her significant haul.

"That's amazing. I love your choices, too, especially the two multi-coloured ones. They remind me of a Mondrian painting. And the faux fur cuffs on this one..."

He held up the jumper that, judging by Becky's earlier comments, was clearly vying for the top spot.

"...is very 'Mad Men' style, and so very you. Just fabulous. Are you going anywhere special today?"

"I am, yes. Mondrian, yes, I thought so too! And the furry cuffs really give off that 'Mad Men' vibe. I've fallen for them. Don Draper would approve."

She batted her eyes at him.

"What am I doing for the rest of the day? Well, I have an important meeting to attend in half an hour, so I'm going to wear this."

She pointed at one of the multi-coloured jumpers he was about to wrap.

"It's too cold to stick with my blouse. I can't talk and shiver at the same time."

Jake nodded. It was another of Becky's habits. When she really fell in love with an item of clothing, she would want to wear it immediately. The cold weather was just an excuse.

"The multi-coloured jumpers and the furry cuffed ones only arrived on Saturday afternoon, just as we were closing. I had a strong hunch they were 'Becky jumpers', which is why I put them on your rail. As you can see, we have very few left in the shop. Kelly is putting in another order as we speak."

Jake handed back Becky's chosen jumper.

"It will look lovely under your jacket, and the brush strokes of pink and blue match your fabulous bag and trainers. Would you like me to wrap your blouse up too?"

"No, just stick it in the bag with the rest of my stuff please, Jake."

Jake pulled a mock startled face.

"There's no 'sticking it in the bag' when *I'm* wrapping! Do you want to keep the jumpers here, and collect them after your meeting, assuming it's local?"

"That would be really helpful, thank you. Yes, please. The meeting is a stone's throw from here, so I'll be back to collect them around 3 o'clock. We can have a proper catch-up then."

Becky was pleased that she'd decided to abandon her smart and silky, but very thin blouse in favour of one of her new jumpers. There was a definite chill in the air, and the last thing she wanted was to deliver a lacklustre talk because she was cold. Besides, it was always nice to wear something she'd just bought.

She emerged from the changing room again, her updated outfit now complete.

"Right, I'll see you later, Jake. Hope the till continues ringing for the rest of the day. As per usual, thank you for your advice and for sorting out those fabulous jumpers for me."

Walking to the venue, Becky felt a mixture of excitement and gratitude. She had butterflies in her stomach. Today was a special day, one she never thought she would see. Here she was, a strong and happy woman, finally at peace with herself and with a life she could never have imagined.

Life had not always been so carefree and happy for Becky, with a generous clothing allowance, designer sunglasses and snazzy jumpers. Far from it.

Becky's mum and dad separated when she was eight years old. It was an extremely acrimonious divorce, with two young children, Becky and her brother Drew, caught in the crossfire of warring parents. Overnight, Becky's little world unravelled, and fear became the driving force in her life. She went from living in a spacious, detached house, on a street with her friends just a few doors away, to a small and cramped bungalow, with her mother and new boyfriend, on the outskirts of the village.

The bungalow only had two bedrooms, so she had to sleep in a tiny conservatory, or rather, a lean-to, which was bitterly cold in the winter. There was only room for a single bed and a small bookcase in her 'bedroom,' which Becky filled with the precious, well-thumbed paperbacks from her favourite authors, Enid Blyton, Lewis Carrol, and JR Tolkien. A lack of space, a cold bedroom, and very few friends to play with were the least of Becky's worries.

Her mother's boyfriend proved to be a bully. He quickly became physically and verbally abusive, and clearly resented the fact that two young children were part of the package that came with his girlfriend. Shouting, swearing, and slapping became the norm, especially for Becky. She lay awake at night, thinking of what she could say, what she could do to please him so the bullying would stop; terrified of what fresh horrors the next day might bring. Her stomach twisted in permanent knots, and at times, she felt completely overwhelmed with anxiety and worry. She tried to become invisible, and retreated to her bedroom to read her books, imagining that she was the central character of each story, and that life was one big, happy adventure.

Inevitably, the relationship between Becky's mother and her boyfriend did not last and within a year of moving into the bungalow, it was all-change again for the three of them. The bullying boyfriend was no longer on the scene, which for Becky was a massive relief. She celebrated his departure in silence, but her problems were far from over.

The next move was to rented accommodation in dire need of modernisation. The previous tenants had removed everything, including door handles and the wall-mounted fires. With money thin on the ground, it took several months before the house resembled anything remotely comfortable and could be described as a home.

The move also meant another new school for Becky, now aged 10. More disruption for a young girl who, despite a fresh beginning, free from her mother's bullying boyfriend, was still spending too much of her time in a state of fear and anxiety.

As a young woman looking back at those early years, Becky felt an immense sadness for the little girl she could still identify with. She was often overlooked by both parents, despite her growing anxiety and the need for reassurance that everything was going to be okay. Her mother was emotionally unbalanced, veering from one toxic relationship to another, while her father had all-but disappeared, moving abroad after the divorce. She saw him just twice a year.

Most of Becky's young life was spent pandering to the whims and impulses of a profoundly insecure mother; trying to please her, sacrificing her own wellbeing and security in the process. 'Why can't I just be a child, and be looked after properly by my mum, instead of me looking after her?' was a recurring thought to which she could find no answer. Although her younger brother was protected largely from their mother's mood-swings and demands, simply because he was a boy, Becky bore the brunt of it all. Every failed relationship, and there were several, resulted in another maternal breakdown and more drama. Unfortunately for Becky, on those occasions, she was the one her mother leaned on.

On the rare times when Becky tried to be assertive, her mother would have nothing of it, and Becky ended up feeling guilty for being a bad daughter. How many times had she apologised to her mother, when it was Becky who was the injured party? An apology from her mother was rare, and that only added to Becky's growing resentment towards her.

As she got older, Becky's coping strategy was to throw herself wholeheartedly into her school work. She excelled at English and History and became the first person in the family to be offered a university place. To her knowledge, she had worked harder than anyone in her year. But it was exhausting, having to perform to a relentlessly high standard at school, while trying to keep her mother emotionally stable. Becky always believed that she had to work much harder than anyone else if she were to succeed at anything. And the extra pressure she put on herself only compounded her anxiety.

Becky deliberately chose a university many miles from her hometown and eventually, after graduation, when the employment offers came flooding in, she picked a job based at the other end of the country. They were important early steps to freedom and independence.

A successful career in advertising followed, but writing was always her true passion. After being told by several clients and friends that she should write a book, Becky decided to do so. And that one book turned into three best-sellers. She had arrived!

Although the relationship with her mother improved over the years, Becky was always grateful for the distance between them. However, with the benefit of experience, and after many hours of soul-searching, Becky was able to see what was behind some of the more troubling aspects of her mother's behaviour.

She too grew up with a demanding mother who made no attempt to conceal the fact that she favoured the younger child. That had always bothered Becky's mother, she spoke about it at length, on many occasions. To compound the feelings of rejection, she walked away from a loveless marriage with little more than her clothes and a small sum from the sale of the family home. In those days, women did not receive an equal share of the proceeds from the house sale. Becky could see that her mother was damaged from her past. However, as Becky observed ruefully, her mother's default position was to blame everyone else for her unhappy life.

Despite success as an author and a businesswoman, Becky remained a troubled woman for many years. The fear and anxiety from childhood exerted a strong grip on her emotions, always in the background, threatening to destabilise her. She recognised that whilst the feelings were indeed a hangover from her childhood, she could not magically wish them away, no matter how hard she tried. There was a limit to what could be accomplished through the many self-help books she had on her bedside table. At the end of every day, she was still alone with her thoughts, and some days those thoughts were too much to bear. Gradually, with the support of her husband and some other special people, she progressed to a happier space, leaving behind most of the demons from her past.

Demons that could have been her undoing, had she not been able to find the help to make significant changes in her life.

Still thinking about her new jumpers, Becky headed to the meeting, walking briskly, a smile on her face. This meeting was one of hundreds she had attended over many years. She felt happy and positive. Life was precious and not something to be taken for granted. The past would never disappear, but it no longer held such a vice-like grip on her emotions and well-being.

Today, Becky was a free woman.

Opening the door, she felt warm air on her face, the central heating was on. No chance of shivering when talking. A good start.

Chairs were arranged in a semi-circle of three rows, with a small table and two chairs at the front of the room. The literature and posters that had played such a big part in her early weeks were in their usual place. They were looking the worse for wear, but it was their messages that mattered.

After helping herself to a peppermint tea, Becky made her way to the small table, and surveyed the room.

Only a few people were sitting down, but the room would soon fill up, it always did. She had time for a little meditation, and to think about what she was going to say. The winter sun, filtered by the paper-thin blinds, cast a kaleidoscope of colours on the surrounding walls. She focussed on them. The patterns mesmerised her; she could lose herself in them.

She felt calm. Everything was in its place, and everything was as it should be.

As the room began to fill, Becky was pleased to see the faces of people she knew so very well. Lots of waves and smiles, and several compliments on her new jumper. There were some unfamiliar faces there, which was always to be expected. A woman in her early twenties gazed at the floor, a pained expression on her face. A very smart, elderly man looked nervous, and a young man sipped his coffee, holding Becky's gaze, smiling back at her. She was really pleased to see Zara looking so well and happy, beaming as always, hugging her cardigan close because the room was still not warm enough for her. There was Lizzie, smiling at her as usual, giving her the thumbs up. They had both joined at the same time.

Becky smiled at every person in the room. She remembered what it felt like in her early days, and how a smile meant so much. She made a mental note to talk to the unhappy looking woman later, and to pass on her contact details.

Taking her place next to Becky, Erica, the secretary opened the meeting by welcoming any new people, encouraging them to listen to the similarities in stories they would hear, not the differences. That always struck a chord with Becky. Such wisdom in so few words. So important to find common ground. Two readings from The Big Book followed, then Erica spoke again.

"I am now handing you over to Becky who has come to share her experience, strength, and hope with us today. Over to you Becky."

Erica smiled.

Placing her watch on the table to ensure she did not run over her time, Becky looked up and began speaking.

"Thank you, Erica. Hello everyone, it's lovely to be here today. My name is Becky, and I'm an alcoholic. Today is an incredibly special day for me, because it's my 20th sobriety birthday. I had my first sober day at this very meeting 20 years ago today, although I'm happy to say the venue has changed. This is much nicer and warmer than the previous meeting room!

It's so lovely to see some of the people here today that helped me to become sober all those years ago, and a few people that I have been privileged to help on their own journey to recovery. I can see some new faces here, too. Welcome. The miracle of recovery is in these rooms, in the fellowship of AA and in AA's 12 steps."

She paused for a few moments, sipping her peppermint tea, taking in the room again, savouring the moment and what it meant to her. AA had saved her life, transformed it, really, and made her the woman she was today. She would be forever grateful to the rooms of AA for giving her a precious second chance to be the person she was destined to be, free from the shackles of her past, free from crippling anxiety and fear. And free from addictive drinking. No need to blot out anything ever again.

"Recovery from alcoholism is just one day at a time, and eventually, the days turn into months and then years. You realise that alcohol no longer dominates your life, and that you can live a happy and fulfilling life without it. Because nothing beats being clean and sober."

"It feels amazing to wake up with a with a clear head, not worrying about who you upset the night before, or obsessing about why you can't stop drinking, despite your best efforts. So, if you're new here today, you're probably feeling overwhelmed and bewildered, just as we all did when we took that first, tentative step to recovery. Please take comfort in the fact that your best years lie ahead of you, and that recovery is possible if you just surrender and become willing to change. Don't forget to grab some phone numbers at the end of the meeting. Recovery from alcoholism begins with one alcoholic talking to another. And if I can do it, then so can you."

"My story starts as a little girl. I was eight when my parents divorced..."

℘

I can be changed by what
happens to me,
but I refuse to be
reduced by it.

Maya Angelou

Chapter 3

Holly

Jake had a real soft spot for Holly. Granted, in the last year she had bought hardly anything on her own; a blouse which she'd subsequently returned, and a pair of trainers. Nothing remotely like the early years when most of her wardrobe came from The Boutique.

In the last 12 months, Jake had become increasingly perplexed by Holly's new 'style' or lack thereof. In the summer, she wore baggy jeans and shapeless t-shirts. In the winter, it was heavy trousers, with lots of layers and huge jumpers. It wasn't so much that the clothes swamped her petite frame, it seemed to Jake that she used the swathes of material in which to hide.

And her coats. Don't get him started on her coats! They were so oversized that she looked bizarre in them, her slender frame disappearing into many folds of dark, coarse fabric. Her long blonde hair, previously all curls and waves, and decorated with Alice bands and ribbons, was scraped back into a severe bun. She had long since stopped wearing makeup.

Whilst she was just as friendly and chatty, Jake sensed an underlying sadness in Holly. Something must have happened to cause such a dramatic change, but he didn't feel it was his place to pry. He didn't want to risk crossing a line and upsetting her.

The only recent time that she had really splashed out was on her birthday last year. And that was down to her overbearing husband, a man to whom Jake had taken an instant dislike. He had made a great show of telling Holly that she could have anything she wanted. Money was no object he'd said, whilst steering her to clothes that he preferred and wanted her to wear, despite her obvious dislike of most of his choices. Jake had also noticed on that occasion, Holly was so much quieter than her usual cheerful self. And since that day, he had not seen her wearing any of those new clothes. However, it was not his place to ask if she had worn them, or more to the point, if she even liked them.

Jake suspected the husband was part of the reason for Holly's change in appearance.

Today, for example, she stood in The Boutique, wearing her warm smile, dressed head to toe in the most awful clothes. It made Jake feel sad.

"Good morning, Holly, how lovely to see you."

Jake wrapped Holly in a hug. He stood back to look at her.

"You're looking different, Holly...can't quite put my finger on it, but you have a glow, and it suits you. Are you just popping in to say hello or has something caught your eye?"

"Hi, Jake, thank you!"

She started to lower her gaze as usual, but then looked right at Jake and smiled.

"Yes, today is a good day for me. I've been admiring that gorgeous jacket in the window, the one that's in the sale."

She pointed at an eye-catching jacket on one of the mannequins.

"I love it, and I'd like to try it on, please. It reminds me of a jacket that I had at university. I wore it until it fell apart. I loved it back then, and this is so similar, it's eerie. If it fits, I'm having it!"

Jake could hardly believe what Holly was saying. This was so different from her recent visits.

But it was great news, a welcome departure from the usual. Looking at the clothing that Holly was wearing, however, it was clear that if the jacket were to do her justice, she would have to try it on with a different pair of jeans and another t-shirt.

He so wanted her to have the jacket.

"Why don't you try it on with these?"

He held up a pair of narrow leg jeans and a close-fit t-shirt.

"You can then see what the jacket looks like in a different outfit..."

Holly completed the sentence for him.

"...rather than this horrendous combination of baggy grey drabness, I know."

She then laughed, pointing at her t-shirt, and tugging at the loose fabric in her trousers.

"Yes. I agree. You know my size. I'll head into the changing room where you can hand me everything."

Five minutes later, Holly emerged from the changing room, doing a little dance and wearing a smile that conveyed her joyful mood. She made her way to the large mirror in between the rails.

"I think it's special to say the least. And the combination with these clothes works so well."

Jake was stunned at her transformation.

"Holly, you look stunning! Where have you been hiding this fabulous figure of yours? The jacket was made for you. It fits in all the right places and is simply perfect for your frame."

"But enough from me..."

Jake made a gesture to indicate he was zipping his mouth.

"...what do you think?"

It was clear, as he looked at Holly's face, what she thought. She was still smiling at herself in the mirror and stroking the jacket.

"I adore it, Jake, and I'll take it, please. I can't afford the t-shirt and jeans today, but hopefully in the next few weeks, I'll be back for those as well. I'm running a bit behind, so if it's all right, can you wrap it whilst I'm changing? Thanks. Oh, and I'm paying cash."

Jake took great care wrapping the jacket. It was exquisite. Dark blue satin, with embroidered flowers, a mandarin collar and a vivid pink lining that matched the trim on the cuffs and collar. It was a million miles away from Holly's current wardrobe and whilst he was curious as to what had prompted the purchase, he thought better of saying anything. She was clearly over the moon with it. Best to leave it at that. He hoped it was the start of something new for her.

Holly walked over to the till with her purse. Jake was surprised when she patiently counted out 40 one-pound coins in silence. Her husband had flashed his Platinum Amex card on her birthday, but there was no sign of that on show today. She was like a child, counting out her pocket money to pay for a special treat.

Jake made a snap decision.

"Actually, Holly, before you came in, I was about to reduce the price of this jacket again. It's the last one in stock, and a small size, which can be hard to sell. So, you can take this back."

He handed her back 20 one-pound coins. Something told him she was going to need the extra money. He knew that Kelly would approve of his decision, too.

"Oh, that's so kind, Jake. Thank you, and what luck!"

Holly's eyes filled with tears which she promptly wiped away using the cuff of her coat.

"So, are you going anywhere special after this, Holly?"

Jake knew what her answer was likely to be, but given the extraordinary nature of this purchase, nothing would surprise him now. Usually, Holly went from The Boutique to the library and then home.

"I'm popping to the library. There are a few things I need to sort out, and then straight back home. I can't tell you how thrilled I am with my jacket, Jake. It means so much to me."

"Well, it's just lovely to see you today as always, Holly. The jacket was made for you."

Jake handed her the bag with the jacket. She hugged it tight to her chest.

"Make sure you team it up with some better fitted clothes. Perhaps with a pair of jazzy heels or some colour matching ankle boots. And send us a picture for our Instagram page."

Holly looked so frail and vulnerable, dressed again in her outsized clothes. It was a poignant moment for Jake. He felt like crying too.

"I will, thank you, Jake. And thank you for making me feel so special. I'll see you soon…and I promise, I will be back for the t-shirt and jeans."

Walking to the library, Holly's head spun in turmoil, fuelled by adrenalin, fear and anxiety. Today was the day for complete and irreversible change. She was no longer going to live a miserable life, weighed down by the unbending rules her husband had imposed so soon into their marriage. And luck had played into her hands today because he had travelled to a conference and was staying overnight. When he returned home tomorrow, Holly would no longer be there.

She viewed her new jacket as a symbol of the life she was going to create without him.

How things had changed in the space of a few months.

Daniel had seemed perfect from their first date. He acted chivalrous, caring, and interested in only her. He asked her questions, showered her with thoughtful gifts and constantly told her how pretty and intelligent she was. So, when he proposed after just six months, there was no doubt in her mind that he was the one.

The first couple of months of their marriage continued in the same vein, but gradually Holly noticed slight changes in Daniel's behaviour towards her. He started asking her not to wear tight jeans or blouses that showed even the slightest bit of cleavage. Then he started telling her what to wear whenever they went out. At first, she looked upon it as a sign that he loved her. It was obvious how much it upset him when other men looked at her. So, she was not surprised when he told her that she should only wear that type of outfit when she was with him. When they did go out, he would have to approve of her outfit.

He would still bring gifts, but the clothes were not her style. Plain mid-length dresses, bulky sweaters that were obviously too big for her, and skirts that had to be taken up at the hem, so she didn't trip on the excess fabric. She hated every item he chose for her. When she plucked up the courage to ask if she could return some of the things she didn't like, he exploded into an expletive littered rant about how ungrateful she was, how it hurt his feelings to think that she didn't want the tokens of his love.

If she loved him, she would wear the clothes he liked to buy for her.

Ever so gently, imperceptibly, he set about breaking the spirit of his self-assured and carefree wife.

Next to face the axe was her job.

He asked her repeatedly why she wanted to work when he could so easily provide for the two of them. He worked long hours at a demanding and stressful job. It didn't make sense for them both to be away from the house all day, he argued. He wanted - needed her to be at home so she could have a meal ready when he returned from work. During the day, she could look after the house, plan meals, and clean; everything a loving wife should expect to do for her husband. It was important for their marriage that their free time was spent enjoying each other's company. Besides, he couldn't bear to think of her coming home on a busy train, especially in the winter, with the evenings closing in.

It was irrelevant that she had undertaken the journey for years without any problems.

After several weeks of being told that if she really loved him, she would stop working and put their marriage first, she handed in her notice, much to the amazement of her colleagues.

Things then began to escalate at an alarming rate.

A few weeks after she resigned, Daniel demanded that she hand over her laptop to him. He said he was concerned that it may have a virus.

Holly did as he asked, but after the initial inspection, daily checks on her laptop began. He would comb through it, often for hours on end.

Then the questions started. Who had she messaged that day? What had she been doing online? Had she bought anything without his permission?

When he discovered a message from an old school friend, he made her life unbearable for weeks, accusing her of having an affair. Holly eventually summoned the courage to tell him that she couldn't put up with this behaviour any longer. If it did not stop, she would leave him.

Then, like the flick of a switch, the charm offensive went into overdrive.

Lovable and adoring Daniel returned, begging her forgiveness, showering her with love and compliments, telling her that he couldn't live without her. He had been under pressure at work, and that had affected his behaviour towards her.

Encouraged and relieved by the intensity of his remorse, Holly forgave him but asked him not to look at her laptop again without her permission. The searches stopped, and Holly saw it as a sign that he once again trusted her. Unbeknown to her however,

Daniel had installed a programme on her machine that gave full remote access to her laptop. He could now check up on her whenever he wanted, from wherever he wanted.

As the months rolled by, Daniel's controlling behaviour resurfaced with a vengeance. He intensified the questioning to interrogation. Who had she seen during the day, and for how long? Had she spoken to anyone in the supermarket or the shopping centre? Had she worn the exact clothes he had told her to wear that day? How much of his money had she spent?

And on it went. The descent into full narcissism was insidious and so subtle that she didn't realise he eroded away her personality little by little, one minuscule slice every single day.

He wanted to know everything about her day in mind-numbing detail. She felt unable to do anything other than conform to his rules and hope for his approval. She could sometimes see what was happening as if in slow motion, but could not find the energy, nor the mental strength to disobey him. By then, he had stopped her from seeing her best friends. Once, during a meal out with a few of Holly's close friends, he had been challenged about his irrational and possessive behaviour.

It had made him incandescent with rage. He told Holly that her friends were a bad influence and wanted to break up their marriage. If she loved him, she would never contact them again.

With Holly's only support network cut off, and her family living halfway around the world, Daniel completed his wife's isolation. The house that she had hoped to turn into a warm and loving home with her kind, thoughtful, attentive husband had become a cold and hostile prison. Holly found that she was no longer 'Holly' with hopes, dreams and aspirations of a great career and wonderful family. Holly had been stripped of her personality and formed into Daniel's wife; a non-entity, his stay-at-home-spouse...drudge.

Shortly after that disastrous and embarrassing meal out, Daniel devised and printed a daily timetable for her. It detailed every task to be completed during the day and, if she had time after the tasks were complete, the safe spaces he allowed her to visit. He demanded to know where she was at any given minute of the day, and would check on her at random times, to make sure, all for her own safety, he claimed. He knew what was best for her. The rigid schedule included a trip to the library, a couple of times a week once she had finished cleaning the house. He told her she was safe at the library, free from the gaze of leering men.

He took full control of their finances, providing her with a small daily allowance. If she wanted to spend any more, she had to ask him, with plenty of notice. He would then decide whether to allow it or not. Holly cringed at the humiliation she faced every month, just to request money for skincare products, deodorant and hygiene items. On more than one occasion, she had been told the money would not be forthcoming, as a punishment for straying from the daily schedule. She resorted to shoplifting. It was a miracle she had not been caught.

The final blow was Holly's mobile phone. Daniel made her delete all her contacts and remove all her social apps. Again, it was for her own good, so she could not be targeted by men with dubious intentions, or by online scammers. What she didn't know was that he had installed an app on her phone that enabled him to track her whereabouts throughout the day.

One extra trip to the library without confessing it, had his mood dominating the evening to the point where Holly believed she was going insane.

Instead of snapping, Holly reached the stage where she followed his routine religiously, and without question. She hid the bouts of tears for fear of further criticism, putting it down to being a bit low, perhaps mildly depressed.

Life with Daniel had become claustrophobic and so miserable that Holly had reached breaking point. She could no longer live in a relationship where everything she did, everything she wore, was controlled by him. How could it have got to this? Every day she asked herself the same question. It felt as though she had sleepwalked from a warm, vibrant, and welcoming room to one that was chilled, bleak and joyless.

Any love she had ever felt for Daniel had long since disappeared. The man she fell in love with had become a narcissistic bully, a man committed to making her life utter misery.

Holly came to loathe him even more than she loathed herself for accepting his abuse and coercion. But she felt powerless, incapable of helping herself out of the mess, unable to do anything. Once a happy, secure and outgoing woman, she was reduced to a barely functioning shadow of her former self.

It had all crept up on her, and now she was trapped inside the prison she once called home.

Holly's escape from her living nightmare ironically started at the library. A poster on the community notice board caught her attention. It advertised an online self-help group for women looking to free themselves from toxic relationships.

The meetings were charity-sponsored and therefore, free to attend. She was wary of using her personal laptop or phone and so signed up for the meetings on one of the library's publicly available computers.

Holly asked one of the assistants at the library if she could join the meetings in a private space because she was anxious not to be overheard or seen by someone who knew her or Daniel. Thankfully, the Librarian was sympathetic to Holly and told her the meetings were always conducted in a small, private room, where a computer was made available to her.

Once a week at midday, Holly joined the support group on Zoom, safe from anyone seeing her. Initially, she was happy simply listening to the women in the group, finding so much common ground in their stories. Soon, though, she began asking questions and started sharing her own experiences, holding nothing back.

These meetings were the making of Holly.

They enabled her to recognise Daniel's nature for what it was. His behaviour was not normal; it was not loving. It was cruel, brutal and cowardly. Most importantly, though, the meetings enabled Holly to start the process of rebuilding her confidence and self-esteem. Rather than simply focussing on Daniel's behaviour, the other women encouraged Holly to realise that she could build a happy and fulfilling life without him. Although she was a victim now, she did not have to continue being one. For the first time in a long time, she started to believe that her life could change.

She had found hope.

With the support of the women, Holly was able to find the strength to begin to reestablish the connection with the woman she had been before Daniel came into her life. At one of the meetings, she was offered practical support in the shape of a place at a women's refuge. She had always thought refuges were only for women who had suffered physical assault but was pleased to discover that they support victims of both physical and mental abuse.

She began to develop a plan, forged with help from the women in the support group and devised under the secrecy of the library computer.

Putting the plan into action was not going to be easy. She was afraid of Daniel's reaction. So, when he told her that he had to attend a conference, a three-hour drive away, Holly saw her window of opportunity.

The magnitude of the day and what lay ahead of her ran through Holly's mind as she said goodbye to Daniel that morning. Previously, some of the women from the support group had shared their breakup traumas in graphic detail. The stories had not been easy to listen to. Holly comforted herself with the fact that Daniel had never come close to being physically violent with her. It helped her focus on the positive steps she was going to take to escape their marriage. Besides, she had given him no reason to suspect that anything out of the ordinary was about to happen. Therefore, he was unlikely to return home unexpectedly. A small niggle in the back of her mind began wearing at her confidence. 'What if he does come back, what if he knows what you're doing, and this is a trap?' The voice, her own voice eroded the hard shell she had built to protect herself since joining the Zoom meetings. It was hard to ignore.

After many encouraging messages from the women at her support group, Holly left the library and headed to her car a little later than usual. She checked her phone before setting off in case Daniel had messaged her during his lunch break. There was nothing. That was a relief. He had, however, told her to check in with him at 3pm on a WhatsApp video call. 3pm was going to be the first break that he would be able to speak to her. The car's clock said it was 1.45pm.

Whatever happened, she had to be on time for that call. If he couldn't get hold of her at the arranged time, she wouldn't put it past him to leave the conference and return home.

Driving home from the library, the weather was dreadful. Lashing rain and spray from the roads resulted in poor visibility. Holly was not surprised that the section of motorway she usually travelled on was closed due to flooding. She had to take a rural route home. Holly's mind turned to the earlier encounter at The Boutique with Jake. Although there was no doubting Jake's kindness, his comment about her fabulous figure had made her feel uncomfortable. If Daniel knew about it, he would be furious with her. Turning everything over in her mind made Holly feel strangely guilty. She wasn't used to getting compliments from anyone other than Daniel. Had she been too relaxed with Jake? Had she been flirtatious with him? Had she been overly enthusiastic when trying on the jacket?

She began to replay the meeting, searching for answers to questions that didn't need asking.

With the weather worsening by the minute, anxiety replaced Holly's feelings of guilt. Whatever happened, she had to be on time and prepared for her 3pm call with Daniel. There was no way she was going to confess her visit to The Boutique.

She had to play it safe and stick to the story she had developed and rehearsed in her mind. She visited the library as usual. She had not spoken to anyone and set off on time. She became delayed because of the weather and the motorway closure. Daniel could not pick holes in her explanation.

She remembered the jacket and took a deep, calming breath.

Pulling into the driveway at 2.40pm, Holly let out a sigh of relief and smiled at herself in the rear-view mirror. There was time to hide her jacket away, mentally compose herself, and be ready and waiting for Daniel, at least five minutes before their call.

The first thing Holly did was to lay the jacket out on their bed so she could admire it for a few minutes. She then hurriedly put it in a drawer for safe keeping. She had an overnight bag packed, hidden at the back of the wardrobe in a place she was sure he wouldn't think to check. She remembered Daniel's reaction when she'd bought a blouse with a voucher from her last employer, without his permission.

He'd cut it into shreds in front of her.

The doorbell rang.

It couldn't be Daniel, surely? He was miles away. And besides, he would just let himself in. There were no scheduled deliveries, no tradesmen due at the house. Daniel only allowed them when he was at home.

Opening the front door a little, Holly was surprised to see two police officers, a man and a woman, standing on the front doorstep, looking serious.

"Mrs Holly Hardwick?"

"Yes. Is everything okay?"

Her mind darted all over the place, then settled on a probable cause for the officers' visit - the elderly neighbour next door, Mavis. Holly had not seen her recently. Did the officers need the key that Mavis had given her for emergencies?

"Can we come inside, please, Mrs Hardwick?"

After showing their ID, the police officers removed their hats and followed Holly into the living room. All seated, with grave expressions, Holly perched on the edge of the armchair by the fire, the police officers on the sofa.

Should she offer them a cup of tea, or just wait and listen to what they had to say? She remained silent.

One of the police officers spoke in a calm manner.

"I'm afraid we must inform you that your husband, Daniel Hardwick, was involved in a road traffic accident earlier today. I am sorry to have to tell you that he died at the scene of the accident."

Holly's head began to spin.

She eventually found her voice, words tumbling out in a rush.

"He's dead? Are you sure he's dead, Daniel Hardwick, my husband? He can't be... I only saw him this morning. That's why I haven't heard from him? Oh my God."

The other police officer spoke.

"I'm afraid so, Mrs Hardwick. Despite the attempts of the paramedics to resuscitate him at the scene of the accident, they were unsuccessful, and he sadly died."

The officer paused. He could see that Holly was struggling to take it all in.

"Is there anything we can do for you? Can we contact a family member or friend to come to the house and be with you?"

The two police officers looked at Holly, quizzically. People reacted to shocking news in many ways. Horror, denial, stunned silence, screaming and sobbing...

They had seen it all.

But the woman in front of them seemed incredibly composed. She was clearly processing what they had told her, but there was no indication of any emotional outburst whatsoever.

Holly stood up and slowly unpinned her hair, to the visible astonishment of the police officers. Masses of blonde waves tumbled down her back. Her mind was still racing. Could it really be true?

"No...no I'm fine. Thank you for your concern, but I don't need anyone to come to the house. I really can look after myself...now."

She glanced at the coat she had been wearing for the past year, draped over the dining room chair. It had engulfed her. That wretched, ugly coat was going to be one of the first things in the charity bag. Followed by the rest of the wardrobe purchased by Daniel.

But before she did any of that, she had a trip to make - to The Boutique - to buy the jeans and t-shirt she had tried on earlier. Jake would be amazed. And she must call the refuge and tell them that she no longer needed a safe place to stay.

Her home was now her sanctuary.

With an expression of serenity on her face, she turned to the police officers.

"Thank you for letting me know about Daniel's death. I suppose at some point, you'll need me to identify the body. I'll wait to hear from you, or the coroner in this matter."

Ten minutes later, Holly closed the front door and made her way up the stairs to take the jacket out of the drawer and place it on the bed, again. She could look at it for as long as she wanted. She then unpacked her overnight bag.

The beautiful new jacket had indeed turned out to be a symbol of the new life that lay ahead of her.

Chapter 4

Amy

A my was a person you just loved being around. She was curious, quirky, and caring. If you were having a difficult day, or just wanted to relax and have fun, Amy was your girl. She always had time for everyone, and possessed a wisdom that far exceeded her 25 years.

And today, as was the case on most days, Amy woke up in a happy mood. Her shift didn't start until 1pm, so she had time to pop into The Boutique and collect the necklace and matching bracelet she'd bought online the night before. Then it was off to work and a chance to catch up with Astrid, something she always looked forward to.

As she drew back the curtains in her bedroom, the sun came flooding in through the window and for a few moments she stood perfectly still, eyes closed, basking in the peace of the morning. She happily allowed her mind to wander.

"Arrgh! I must ring Sarah!"

Amy's Zen state of mind ended abruptly.

She began a frantic search for her mobile phone and found it tucked underneath her pillow, along with two baking books. So that explained the crick in her neck this morning. Thankfully, she was not late for the call. Who was calling who? She couldn't remember. Best that she be the one to make the first move.

"Hi Sarah! So, tell me, am I to be baking brownies until the early hours, or staring forlornly into my empty mixing bowls?"

Amy could barely contain her excitement.

"Good morning, Amy. Well, I was about to ring you as we had agreed, but you seem to have beaten me to it."

"Ahh, sorry but I just can't stand the suspense!"

Amy laughed apologetically.

"Well, I am the bearer of good news, great news in fact. Our customers loved your brownies. The vegan versions went in the first hour, swiftly followed by the gluten free and dairy options. Every customer bought more than one, and they really loved that we were offering vegan and gluten free choices.

Honestly, it was the best reaction we've ever had to new bakes. You should be pleased with yourself. We are!"

"Oh my, that's fantastic news, Sarah! I'm so excited, and thank you, what fabulous feedback. I do love baking brownies! If you could see me right now, I'm punching the air and standing on one leg. My cat thinks I've lost the plot!"

"Well, we don't want you to come to any harm, Amy, because we're placing a large order for six of our cafes. If your brownies always sell as quickly, we plan on rolling them out across all 40 of them. However, we would need to discuss this with you, because you must be able to bake substantial quantities at short notice. But that's something for later. For now, let's proceed with the order for the six cafes."

Amy did not know where to put herself. She felt like skipping around the lounge squealing, but she had to get a grip on herself. Pizzie, her cat, seemed most perturbed.

What a vote of confidence for her baking skills. Her mind whirled with shopping lists and thinking about the time she would need to set aside in the next week to bake, on top of her full-time job.

"This is all beyond amazing, Sarah. What quantities are we looking at for your six cafes?"

"Well, I've done the sums, and we'd like to order 216 brownies in total. That's 36 brownies per cafe, 12 vegan, 12 dairy and 12 gluten free. And we need the brownies to be delivered to each cafe next Thursday morning between 6am and 9am. I'll send over the purchase order with all the details in a few minutes, but before I do, can you bake and despatch this order on time?"

Amy felt as though she was going to faint on the spot. What would Astrid make of this huge win? She would be thrilled for her.

Despite feeling that at any given moment her legs were going to buckle beneath her, Amy made a conscious effort to adopt a more serious and professional tone.

Stop behaving like an excitable five-year-old. Be cool, be calm, be collected, whatever that means. And breathe. Just sit down and focus.

"That's no problem at all, Sarah. I can easily set aside the time to fulfil your order. Just send me over the paperwork and I'll start making the necessary preparations."

Amy surprised herself at how fast she became composed. It helped that she was no longer balancing on one foot, and perplexing Pizzie.

After the conversation with Sarah ended, it was time to make plans.

Ingredient shopping could wait for a few days, and she could order the extra baking tins and packaging online later this afternoon or, after her shift if she ran out of time. It would take her a couple of days to prepare, bake and pack the order, but thankfully, she had some annual leave to take. She could think about the bigger potential order after this one had been completed.

But back to earth for a minute, she had to get on with her day. First thing was off to The Boutique to collect her order, and hopefully have the chance of a brief chat with Kelly. Amy was inspired by Kelly and how she had built The Boutique from a market stall, whilst bringing up her son alone.

As things calmed down, Amy felt her Zen-like state gradually returning. And slowly, an overwhelming feeling of gratitude washed over her.

As she looked around the lounge, the modest disarray confronting her pleased her. The velvet scatter cushions lay on the sofa in a haphazard manner, two of them partially hidden by an oversized fluffy throw she had recently bought. The morning sun highlighted the thin film of dust on her laptop screen. Last night's empty coffee cup sat on the side table.

She could see the ring stain from where she had put it down absent-mindedly, her head filled with business planning and recipes.

But the biggest crime of all, were her trainers. They were still by the front door where she had left them without undoing the laces.

Quelle horreur!

Amy had half an hour before she needed to leave, so she wandered into the kitchen to make a fresh cup of coffee.

The kitchen was the one room in the house that was always spotlessly clean and very well organised. Matching glass jars of dry ingredients stood in line like soldiers on the stainless-steel shelves, each one carefully labelled with their use by date. Gleaming utensils, polished to perfection, each one in its rightful place, filled the lined drawers. Her beloved baking tins, stacked precisely according to size and use, nestled in the cupboard dedicated to them; a measured disc of greaseproof paper separating each one.

Amy's kitchen looked primed and ready to whirr into action for the next big bake. She looked upon her pristine little kitchen as a testing ground before the next move, a purpose-built bakery, where space was not an issue, and she could bake every single day.

Back in the lounge, coffee in hand, Amy smiled sadly to herself.

At her family home, this array of coffee stains and dusty laptops would have been declared a major contamination hazard by her mother, leading to multiple corrective actions involving bleach and disinfectant in copious quantities. Living by Amy's house code, the tidying up could wait until the evening or more likely, the next day. She was now a free spirit, released from the rituals and regulations enforced by her mother, aided and abetted by her hapless father. Amy left the family home aged just 16 and was no longer governed by them.

Amy's childhood had been dominated by a multitude of unfathomable and unbending rules, created and monitored by her mother. Life in all its glorious, multi-coloured and imperfect facets only began for Amy once she packed her last suitcase and walked out of the front door.

Amy grew up in a household in which her mother's compulsive behaviour was a corrosive thread that ran through every aspect of daily living. All day every day, 365 days a year.

Amy remembered being a young girl; she witnessed her mother washing her hands repeatedly throughout the day. She demanded that Amy followed suit. Initially, Amy had not questioned her mother, but as the years rolled by, she became increasingly perplexed by the unrelenting need for cleanliness.

The house was always immaculate, resembling a show home; her mother rearranged the furniture every morning at the same time. Neither Amy nor her father were allowed to move anything, not even by a centimetre. To avoid her mother's censure, both would choose to sit on the carpet. Transparent plastic sheets covered the sofa and chairs, and the side tables were also protected by a thin film of plastic. Any attempts by Amy to challenge the situation, no matter how gently she raised the subject, were met with obstinacy and dismissal.

Her mother would refuse to be drawn into any discussion, or to accept any form of reasoning.

It drove Amy mad.

She loved her mother, but any warmth or affection she felt towards her was gradually replaced by resentment, dislike, and frustration.

Drinks and meals were consumed in the kitchen, with the emphasis on eating tidily, not socialising. The crockery and cutlery had to be hand-washed before being placed in the dishwasher, where it was washed on two cycles. The sink was then bleached, and the kitchen surfaces and doors disinfected. The ritual was performed several times throughout the day, from early morning to late at night. Leftovers were disposed of immediately, wrapped in several bags before being placed in the refuse bin. Amy's mother was terrified of anything that could attract rodents or contaminate the home.

It all added up to a growing list of mundane and repetitive tasks, which Amy had to share with her mother as she grew older. There were many times when Amy felt like sabotaging the routines, or simply disregarding them, but she always held back, fearful of how her mother would react.

As a young girl, Amy would have loved to be able to invite her friends over for a sleepover or to listen to music in her room. It was out of the question, of course. Consequently, she began to retreat into her bedroom where her love of music blotted out what was happening around her.

When she was 14, Amy began to assume the responsibility for cooking, under the watchful eye of Mother. Every meal was bland and boring with little seasoning. And snacks were forbidden. The mere thought of crumbs on the floor or furniture was enough to send Mother into a state of panic. Amy relished the times when she could go out with her friends and eat pizza and ice cream sundaes. At the back of her mind, however, was the fear that if she ever threw up due to overeating, Mother would become completely unhinged. Sometimes it was not worth the risk, and so occasionally she would make an excuse and join her friends after they had eaten.

Over the years, Amy's resentment towards her mother grew. Every fibre of her being cried out to leave home; but she was still too young to do so.

Amy had few memories of her grandma and aunt visiting the house. Spontaneous visits were always discouraged. Mother required time to mentally prepare for guests 'messing up' her home, and then became exhausted at the idea of having to perform an intensive clean after they had left. Besides, who in their right mind would want to spend their time visiting when they had to sit on plastic covered furniture and were offered no refreshments other than water?

Eventually, visits dried up because Mother could not cope with the trauma and the increased workload.

By the time Amy reached the age of 15, she found it impossible to tolerate any aspect of her mother's behaviour and was challenging her and her father regularly. There was no love left in Amy's heart for either of them. She began to look upon the passing of every day as another day nearer to when she could leave.

With no siblings she felt increasingly alone in the sterile and peculiar environment.

A significant bone of contention for Amy were the school visits, or rather lack of them. Parent evenings had long since been out of the question for her mother. The thought of sitting in a hall full of parents and children, many coughing and sneezing, terrified her. Consequently, the task of talking to the teachers about Amy's progress fell at her father's feet. Eventually, he too stopped any physical contact with the school, due to his wife's overbearing anxiety. Amy felt incredibly resentful and hurt at his decision. She had seen him as her only support in the house, but now realised that enabling her mother, keeping her happy and stable, was more important to him than she was.

She felt embarrassed and awkward having to explain to her teachers why neither of her parents would be attending the latest parent evening. There were only so many times she could make excuses for them. In the quiet of her bedroom, her emotions alternated between rage and despair. It became clear that her mother's obsessiveness came before anything.

It had also become obvious to Amy that Mother was not going to improve. Any attempts by Amy or her father to get her help through therapy were stonewalled. Amy became resigned to the fact that this infuriating woman would never be able to live a happy and normal life. Nor would she acknowledge the impact that her actions had on Amy. And as for Amy's father, it was anything for a quiet life, or so it seemed.

Ironically, of the three of them, Amy was the only one to attend counselling sessions. With the support of her form tutor at school, she had suggested to both parents that some sort of therapy could help the situation at home. The suggestion, although tactfully made, was met with customary hostility. Her father, as usual, fell in line with his wife.

Increasingly angry and isolated, Amy signed up for a course of six counselling sessions shortly after her 15th birthday. By providing her with several coping strategies, Amy's counsellor helped her to progress beyond shouting at her mother and seething inwardly in her bedroom, and she was able to navigate a life that was anything but normal. In later years, Amy credited the counselling for helping her to get through the final year at home. She could not, however, bring herself to feel any sympathy or empathy towards her mother or father. Any residual love for them had been snuffed out years before.

Amy had been biding her time, and when she reached her 16th birthday, it was time to leave.

Salvation came in the form of her aunt who suggested that Amy move in with her. It was an offer that Amy was pleased and relieved to accept. Her aunt had been a witness to Amy's suffering for many years. She knew her sister had little, if any, hope of an imminent recovery from the obsessions that consumed her every waking moment and had been noticeable in childhood.

Although relieved to see Amy go, Mother nonetheless made a fuss when Amy told her she was leaving. In truth, having a teenage daughter with a mind of her own and now openly questioning her rules, had become incredibly tiresome and wearing. The joy Amy experienced as she emptied her bedroom, one bag at a time, was unbridled. She felt liberated.

Amy wanted germs, she wanted mess, she wanted pizza. Life was out there waiting for her. And Amy was ready to run towards it with open arms.

She would never return to the family home.

Leaving home enabled Amy to flourish, and little by little, she began to heal from her upbringing. It was at her aunt's house that she discovered a real talent for baking. Thankfully, her aunt was completely different to her mother. In her house there were very few restrictions, and she was quite happy for Amy to spend hours in the kitchen, baking - making as much mess as she wanted. Every day, a new cake or pastry would be served up to enthusiastic recipients.

A few years later, Amy was able to move into her own flat. How she loved living in a home where untidiness was not frowned-upon, and cleaning up was undertaken when she felt like it. A house could be lived in very happily without any restrictions. Although fully employed as a manager at a local café, Amy's enthusiasm for baking only increased once she had her own kitchen. Within a few months of the move, she was not only providing cakes to her aunt and uncle, but she was also supplying sweet treats to a few local independent cafes. It snowballed from there.

Amy's current exuberant mood continued, buoyed by the earlier phone call with Sarah. It was not lost on her that after years of preparing the most insipid and unimaginative meals, she was planning on launching a bakery, where the only limit on what she could bake was her imagination. She had an abundance of creative ideas, and Sarah's order could not have come at a better time.

Although Amy's new business was still at the embryonic stage, she had been gaining practical experience of baking to order. She believed that after today's order, there was no time like the present to officially launch her baking business.

She looked forward to catching up with Astrid later, after work. Amy wanted to share her ideas for new cakes and plans to promote her new business. Not forgetting to relay, in minute detail, *that* earlier phone call. It had been a few weeks since the two women had last met, but in the meantime, Amy had been following Astrid's advice to the letter. When you were given the gift of mentorship by someone as successful and experienced as Astrid, you did not turn it down. And you did exactly as she suggested. Astrid and Amy had met by chance at the café that Amy managed. She had been mesmerised by the sophisticated woman. Astrid exuded the understated elegance of a wealthy woman, while radiating an aura of poise and confidence. Far from being aloof, she was chatty and curious, warm and friendly. Within a few weeks, Astrid had begun to seek Amy out for a coffee and a chat, which invariably continued after Amy's shift had ended.

After several weeks of getting to know one another, Amy tentatively sharing her ideas for starting a bakery, Astrid, had offered to be her business mentor.

Astrid, an incredibly successful and accomplished businesswoman! Amy was inspired and awestruck by everything Astrid had achieved in her illustrious career, but it was her upbringing that made her so warm and approachable. If Astrid could be a success, there was a good chance that Amy could too.

Yes, she was going to enjoy seeing Astrid later.

The Boutique was looking especially inviting and appealing today.

Kelly had styled the window with an autumnal theme, and was in the process of dressing three mannequins with her usual flair and eye for colour when Amy walked in.

"Hello Amy, you've caught me in the act! I've been sidetracked from window dressing by customers that have been coming in after yesterday's Instagram video. No complaints of course!"

Kelly stepped out of the window.

As usual, she had that fresh-from-the-catwalk look.

She was dressed in a caramel-coloured bias-cut satin skirt, with an oversized, charcoal grey, fine-knit jumper, cinched at the waist with a silver raffia belt. Her accessories were bold too, several mixed-metal bracelets on both wrists, and a long string of pearls in cream, black and pink cascaded down her jumper. The gold velvet Alice band did a good job of pulling back her thick wavy hair, revealing large silver earrings, studded with crystals, which complemented the pearl necklace. The outfit was finished off with her trademark biker boots. On Kelly, everything looked fabulous and artfully composed.

She was the ultimate model for The Boutique.

"I've got your necklace and matching bracelet, nicely gift wrapped, in the back. Then I thought, what if she wants to try them on first?"

She removed the necklace and the bracelet from one of the mannequins.

"Happy days, I have the same ones here."

Amy tried them on, checking the mirror to ensure they looked as good on her as they did on the mannequin.

"The window is your best yet, Kelly. And I really like

these. Perfect for the dress I bought from here a few weeks ago. I'm of a mind to come back later in the week and try on that glamorous blouse."

She pointed to a Gucci-inspired blouse in striking shades of terracotta, green and pink. It looked divine; with a dramatic pointed collar, and billowing sleeves that gathered in to a long, slim cuff.

"Well, don't leave it too long. I only have three left in stock. I don't think they'll be here tomorrow. Shall I put one aside for you?"

Kelly was always one heartbeat away from her next sale.

"Yes please, in medium. Thank you. I can't stop today, so that would be perfect."

Amy's earlier news occupied her mind and there were no signs of it departing imminently. She was finding it hard to focus on anything other than brownies and baking. That blouse had caught her eye, though, and thinking about the launch of her bakery, it would look so stylish and eye-catching in the photographs.

However, she had no time for chit chat this morning. There were brownie bakes to plan, even more tins to buy, and a baking empire to build. Thankfully, as

Kelly was in the middle of dressing three immodest mannequins, the feeling was mutual. They could catch up later.

Amy left The Boutique with an hour to spare before her shift started. She would use that precious 60 minutes to trawl the internet, looking for cake tins and packaging materials. What a blissful way to spend an hour!

The tidying up was for another day.

The café was bustling when Amy walked in. The staff were busy too, clearing tables, serving customers, restocking cutlery, but always with a smile. Amy always impressed upon each one of them the importance of a smile, even when it was not reciprocated. It had taken a while for it to sink in, but the café had become renowned for its great customer service as well as its decent coffee.

Seema, the team leader interrupted Amy, just as she was about to regale her with the news of her earlier order. It was still there, top of mind.

"Hi, Amy. There's a guy over there wants to speak to you."

She pointed to the two comfortable armchairs at the back of the café.

"He's not been waiting long. About 10 minutes I'd say."

Amy walked over to the man. She didn't recognise him. He was very good looking and dressed in clothes that, although casual, were unmistakeably expensive. He glanced at Amy as she approached but remained seated.

He didn't look at all happy.

"Hi, I'm Amy. I understand you'd like to speak to me?"

He nodded.

"I would, yes. Is it okay if you sit down, please?"

It seemed a little formal, being asked to sit down by a stranger in the café she managed, but she sat as requested, looking at him nervously.

Why was he here?

"I'm Astrid's son, Steven. I know you were supposed to be meeting Mum later today."

He paused, taking a deep breath.

"I'm so sorry to have to tell you this, but we lost Mum last week. She died in her sleep."

Amy's mouth dropped open in disbelief.

"She died? Astrid...Astrid died? That can't be right. Oh, my word. She looked so well...I can't believe it. She was so chatty and so...full of life when we last met."

Aware that she was gabbling, Amy stopped talking. Her mind was in a blur with the unexpected and truly shocking news. There had been no sign that Astrid was unwell at any of their meetings. It didn't make sense. Despite wanting to bombard Steven with questions, she realised that the middle of a busy café was neither the right place, nor the right time. Steven softened his tone, sensing Amy's shock and upset.

"We're having a celebration of Mum's life in a few weeks. I hope you can come. I know she would want you to. I'll send you the details. Mum was fond of you, Amy. She spoke about you often, and of how much she enjoyed your mentoring sessions. You reminded Mum of herself as a young woman. I know this is all very unexpected. I hope this helps."

He handed Amy a letter with her name on the envelope, written in Astrid's neat handwriting.

"It's best that you read it at home, I think."

They stood up. Amy felt awkward until Steven embraced her, tears streaming down both their faces.

"I would very much like to come to the celebration of Astrid's life."

Amy paused, gathering her breath, and wiped away her tears.

"She was such a wonderful woman. She helped me so much. I can't tell you how fond of her...I was. Thank you for this, Steven. I'll read it later."

She was about to add that she was sorry for his loss but thought better of it. It always seemed such a trite thing to say in the circumstances.

At home, Amy found herself thinking about Astrid into the early hours of the morning. Her exciting news from yesterday now seemed so unimportant, even trivial. It was from another world, one that seemed so out of reach. At least that was how she felt. In such a short space of time, Amy had experienced emotions at both ends of the scale, absolute joy, and utter, heartbreaking grief. How could Astrid be dead? She was a one-off. An amazing woman. Amy felt that life was never going to be the same again.

Amy's mood then began to dip further. Could she really move ahead with her new business without

Astrid in the wings to advise her? She felt lost and unsure.

And desperately sad.

"Astrid's letter...how on earth could I have forgotten about it?"

Amy's sudden outburst startled Pizzie who until now, had been sleeping peacefully in her lap. She reached into her bag and carefully opened the envelope, removing its contents.

What Amy read would change her life forever.

The magnitude of Astrid's intentions was, at times, too much for Amy to grasp. It was beyond generous. Despite her immense sadness, Amy could not help but be excited, and she began to visualise her new business. She resolved that tomorrow was a day for action. She would kickstart the business plan that she had carefully crafted with Astrid. She had the brownie order and now, Astrid's overwhelming vote of confidence.

It was time to get things moving. Empress Bakery. The name had a nice ring to it. She was sure that Astrid would approve.

❧

In order to be
irreplaceable one must
always be different.

Coco Chanel

Chapter 5

Astrid

A strid commanded attention wherever she went. And today was no exception.

Dressed in a Chanel suit accessorised by Prada glasses, a vintage Birkin bag, a Cartier watch, gifted to her under scandalous circumstances, and several Tiffany bangle bracelets dangling from one slender wrist, she attracted glances and admiring stares. As usual though, she was oblivious to any of this, focussing intently on getting to The Boutique before it closed. Astrid was on a mission to buy velvet purses. Nothing could stop her.

"It's just down here, Astrid, I can see it."

Her chauffeur, Tom, pointed down the alleyway in front of them to a large shop, festooned with twinkling fairy lights.

"I'll get the car, so you don't have to walk back to the car park."

Astrid appreciated having a chauffeur. It seemed indulgent, but she simply hated driving. Once she reached the age of 60, a chauffeur became one of life's little luxuries. Now, 10 years down the line, and Tom was not only the perfect chauffeur, in Astrid's eyes, but also a person she could trust without hesitation. He was a kind and sensible soul, and he looked after Astrid very well. And Tom loved the job of taking this exceptional woman out on her many and varied trips.

Astrid was relieved to reach The Boutique and discover it was open. It closed at 5pm not 4pm as she had initially thought. She hated rushing. Being busy was one thing, chasing your tail like a mad fool was another.

Opening the door to the pleasing sound of light jazz music, she immediately became enchanted by the vibrant colours and the dazzling array of jewellery, bags and clothes.

'Clearly the owner knows how to buy for the changing seasons, and how to dress this window,' she thought.

Everything fitted so well together, to create a magical and quite extraordinary patchwork of colours and textures. While she could see the influence of the catwalk in many of the pieces, the spacious, dramatically lit shop was clearly a fabulously eclectic and indulgent space for women of all ages to enjoy.

A few pieces had already caught her eye, but that was for another day, when she would ask Amy to accompany her.

"Hello. I'm here for velvet purses!"

Jake spun round.

"Good afternoon. Oh, I do love your vintage Birkin, and your Chanel suit is just...gosh, words fail me. You look so elegant. And those mesmerising bracelets..."

Jake moved out from behind the counter to admire Astrid more closely.

Astrid was pleasantly surprised with Jake's effusive greeting and his compliments. It was rare indeed for people to be so openly complimentary, but then Amy had told her a bit about Jake and how, before joining The Boutique, he had worked at Dior. He clearly had an eye for the finer things.

"Oh, thank you. I do love my clothes and my accessories."

She patted her bag.

"And whilst today, as you can see, I am supporting the fashion houses of Paris and Milan, tomorrow you will find me wearing an outfit, top to toe, from an upcoming British designer. I like to support home grown talent too. And I'm one of those women who plans what she is going to wear a week ahead."

Astrid beamed at Jake.

"I find it saves so much indecision and faffing around. Time is so very precious. I don't want to squander mine."

Jake loved her response to his compliment, and he was on a roll.

"Well, I must say, you look incredible. You could have come straight out of the pages of Vogue."

He stepped back from Astrid to allow her space to browse, even though he wanted nothing more than to talk with her at length, and to discover more about her style. He was also more than just a little curious to find out which British designers she favoured. However, she was clearly focussed on one important task, and given this was their first encounter, he felt it was inappropriate to be overly familiar.

Back to business. He pointed to the mirrored glass shelves beside the two armchairs.

"You mentioned purses, and we have a lovely selection in five different patterns. As you can see they are so pretty, made with cotton velvet, and the beads are hand-sewn into intricate patterns of flowers, hearts, stars and butterflies."

He handed Astrid two of the purses so she could examine them more closely.

"The lining is in colour matching cotton. Even better, every purse is Fairtrade."

Within the space of 30 seconds, she had made her decision.

"They are just what I envisioned, perfect in fact. I would like 20 of them, in every design you have."

She handed the purses back to Jake, waving her hand airily at the shelves which were soon to be cleared of every single purse.

"And would you be able to tissue wrap them individually for me please? They are gifts for the volunteers in a charity I support. Amy has told me about your gift-wrapping skills."

Astrid smiled at Jake who bowed at the compliment.

"It would be my pleasure. It will take me a good half-an-hour. I don't know if you have any shopping to do, but you're more than welcome to wait here."

He gestured to one of the armchairs.

"And you know Amy?"

"Yes, I do. She's a wonderful girl. So much talent."

She paused for a moment. The thought of going out into the chilly air again only to come back in 30 minutes was not in the least bit appealing.

"I'm happy to wait here and chat with you. Why don't I ask my chauffeur, Tom, to bring us a coffee. What would you like?"

Jake was touched by her thoughtful and kind gesture.

"A caramel latte would be perfect, thank you."

He decided not to ask any more questions about the connection between Amy and Astrid. He sensed that she did not want to be drawn any further on the subject.

"If we are to drink coffee together, I must know your name."

Jake came towards Astrid, arm outstretched to shake her hand.

"I'm Jake and I manage The Boutique."

"Hello Jake, I am Astrid."

In the 30 minutes they shared their coffee, with Jake busy wrapping every purse to his usual exacting standards, Astrid chatted about the charity she supported and how most of her time was spent working on charitable causes. She also expressed interest in Jake's experience at Dior, inviting him to look more closely at her Chanel suit. But only after she had paid for the purses. She liked to do things in a precise and ordered manner.

"Thank you, Jake, it has been lovely meeting you. And if your gift wrapping is anything to go by, I can see why you won a scholarship with Dior. The little tissue wrapped packages are sublime, and I know they will be very well received by the volunteers. You are a perfectionist. Ahh, I see Tom is here now."

She gestured to the door where Tom waited patiently to escort her back to the car.

"I will say my goodbyes now."

She turned to leave The Boutique.

Jake made it to the door just in time to open it for her.

"So lovely to meet you too, Astrid. And don't be a stranger. I'm sure that Kelly, the owner of The Boutique, would like to meet you. We may even be able to tempt you with some of the pieces from our British designers. Our aim is to offer customers beautiful and unusual garments and accessories."

Astrid nodded her head in agreement.

"I will most definitely come back. Thank you for the invitation."

And in seconds, she was gone, disappearing into the alleyway, leaving a hint of the lingering fragrance; Miss Dior Eau De Parfum behind her.

Astrid's life had not always been a merry-go-round of designer clothing, charity work and chauffeurs. In fact, her upbringing was in sharp contrast to the life she now enjoyed. Originally from a small mining town in the north of England, she grew up in a loving family with two siblings, an older sister, and a younger brother. Her parents adored one another, and there was always more than enough love for all three children to feel secure and cherished.

Money was thin on the ground, however.

Her mother juggled three jobs; a dinner lady and cleaner by day, then stuffing small plumbing parts into envelopes by night, a task she eventually roped her children into. The pay was poor, but it was home-based work, and it was regular. It also meant that the children were not left at home alone when their father was on a late shift. He worked in a warehouse, but any hopes of promotion were dashed when he was injured in an accident on the premises. Today he would receive compensation for the injuries which were due to workplace negligence, but in those days, he was lucky to keep his job. Consequently, until his death, he struggled with chronic pain.

Whilst Astrid had fond memories of her childhood, especially the family holidays which were budget breaks in a small caravan at the seaside, one thing she did not enjoy was having to wear her sister's old clothes.

That could account for her later love of fashion and designer labels.

As a young girl, having to wear washed-out, faded blouses with scratchy collars, and too-short jeans, lengthened with any spare piece of fabric her mother could lay her hands on...just the thought of it made her cringe. How many times had she prayed that her sister would have a growth spurt, so the hand-me-down clothes would fit and not be so clearly well-worn? However, apart from spending her early years in clothes that she didn't like and didn't fit properly, her childhood memories were happy ones.

She was ecstatic when her mother announced they had been awarded a small sum of money, in the form of a grant for new school uniforms. For all three of them. The money even stretched to new shoes, which for Astrid, was Heaven. No girl had ever been so excited to visit a shop and pick out new blouses, jumpers, skirts and shoes for school! Granted, they were not as fashionable as those being worn by the girls from homes where money was not a problem, but Astrid loved her new shoes and took great care of them. The slightest scuff on the shoes or tear in her uniform was cleaned or mended immediately. Astrid was keen to ensure that her school uniform remained in pristine condition for as long as possible. There was no guarantee that the money would be forthcoming again.

At school, Astrid excelled in needlework and textiles. Give her a pattern, a needle and a piece of cloth, and she would spend hours creating a garment, bag or accessory that was so striking, it would not look out of place in a glossy fashion magazine.

She loved visiting charity shops for unusual and beautiful clothes which she then took apart and refashioned, or simply restored to their former glory. Always with the aim of selling them on, so she could have some money of her own. Every penny from her Saturday job, working at the local dry cleaners, went on fabric and second-hand clothes. Ironic for a girl that did not like her sister's hand-me-downs.

Seeing her daughter's talent in action, Astrid's mother enlisted her support with the clothes that wealthy customers gave her to mend, or spot clean. Astrid was in her element. She repaired torn linings, so they looked like new. Jewelled buttons and satin trims would enhance a drab looking dress. Stains on expensive clothing disappeared as if by magic, without damaging the fabric, or leaving a tell-tale ring behind.

Nothing phased Astrid.

Her invisible stitching proved to be a Superpower, and news of her magical fingers spread. Her mother had long since given up the pretence that she was the genius behind the dramatic renovations. She brought home garment after garment for her daughter to repair, from every home she cleaned. And everyone knew that Astrid was behind the work.

Buoyed by the demand for her services, Astrid started putting aside most of the money she earned, for a special purpose. A plan took shape in her mind, helped by regular trips to the library, where she had a keen interest in business plans and starting a business. She knew how much money affluent women were willing to spend on keeping their treasured pieces looking immaculate and fresh. They did not question her prices.

At the age of 18, Astrid knew her own worth. Undercharging was not something she could ever be accused of.

So, her parents were not in the least bit surprised when Astrid announced that she would be moving her home business to a more official footing, taking on her own premises, offering spot cleaning for garments, and specialising in alterations for designer brands and vintage clothing. Her experience of the previous five years, and belief in her own talent gave her the confidence to make the bold move. She found a small shop, prepared a business plan, knew which equipment she had to buy, and had saved enough money to get started.

The missing piece of the jigsaw, money to create a unique and inviting space, came from an unexpected quarter. One of Astrid's more affluent customers offered an interest free loan. It was enough for Astrid to be able to give the shop an upmarket look and feel, with luxurious decorations and upholstered chairs made from the most sumptuous fabric, for when customers wanted to wait and chat. And the customers kept on coming, recommending the shop to their friends and family. Within a few years, she had paid off the loan and had added dry cleaning to her services.

Astrid's approach proved to be a winning formula, one that was the making of her.

25 years later, she sold Empress Alterations and Dry Cleaning, a national chain, for several million pounds. Other successful business ventures followed, until she decided to wind-down all her business commitments and focus on one of her real passions - mentoring women who were looking to start their own business.

Back home, in her study, fresh from 'bulk buying' velvet purses, Astrid was in a reflective mood. Life had undoubtedly been good to her. The pursuit of great wealth and material possessions had never been her prime motivation, but she nevertheless loved the freedom that money had given her. And the fact that it enabled her to help others. Her thoughts turned to Jake and their earlier encounter.

What a great character, and so kind to her. She loved meeting interesting and enthusiastic people.

"Time for tea!"

Bobbie, the housekeeper interrupted Astrid's thoughts and brought in a tray of tea and cake - a large mug of tea and a slice of her favourite cake - coffee and walnut, courtesy of Amy. It was the last piece.

"Ahh, that's so nice of you, Bobbie, thank you. Just what the doctor ordered. Or perhaps not, given the circumstances!"

Bobbie placed the tray on the coffee table beside Astrid's desk.

"I'll put the main light on, Astrid. It's quite dark in here. You don't want to strain your eyes, because it will give you a headache, and we don't want that!"

She patted Astrid's arm.

Astrid wondered how she had ever coped without

Bobbie. Certainly, in the last few years, her reliance on the capable, loyal, and cheery woman had grown. Bobbie and Tom were the only people outside of her immediate family that knew about her health.

"Bobbie, have you ever been to The Boutique? I was in there this afternoon, buying velvet purses."

Astrid gestured to the white carrier bag on the sofa, its contents awaiting distribution in the morning.

"I was quite taken with it, more so than I expected. Some stylish items. Really friendly and chatty manager too. I think I'll pay them a return visit in the next week or so. I have my eye on a few nice scarves, even a jacket!"

Bobbie nodded.

"I've bought a few jumpers from there, but nothing recently. You've given me a nudge to call in on my next day off. Now, I'll be downstairs, defrosting the alleged frost-free freezer. If you need anything, just call."

After a short break enjoying Amy's cake, Astrid began to write, occasionally breaking off, lost in her own thoughts. This evening, thoughts kept returning to her health. The headaches had become more persistent in the last few weeks, a nagging ache at the back of her head, just where the aneurysm in her brain was located.

The operation seven years before had saved Astrid's life. It was a remarkably close call. A coil had been fitted around the aneurysm to stop the flow of blood from expanding it. Despite the operation being declared a success by her medical team, Astrid knew there remained a significant risk that the aneurysm could burst at any time. She had been told this by several consultants. And recently, her headaches had become much more regular and persistent, with the one that she was now experiencing, one of the worst to date. Strong painkillers were not even taking the edge off it. She had an appointment with her consultant in a few days, but another operation was out of the question. Medical science had accomplished everything that it could for Astrid, so, other than monitoring the aneurysm, it was a case of living life and eating healthily, with cake, of course, in moderation.

"Ah well, what will be, will be."

She removed her watch, rubbing her thumb over the inscription before gently placing it on her desk. The words had faded a little, but they were etched on her heart indelibly. How she had adored him. He was the love of her life, the one that got away; the one that *had* to get away. Of course, the feeling was mutual.

He was absolutely besotted with her. Every few days that summer, she had received an exquisite written note or letter from him, occasionally with flowers, but always a dab of his after shave on monogrammed paper – no signature, only his initial. She kept these precious declarations of love in one of her jewellery boxes, safely tucked away in the bottom drawer of her desk, for her eyes only.

It was sadly a love that could never live beyond a few months, cloaked in secrecy and subterfuge as it was. Whispered conversations on the phone, clandestine meetings in opulent, remote hotels, miles away from his ancestral home; always the lingering fear they would eventually be caught, or rather, *he* would be caught out. And that could not happen, because he would lose everything, his royal status the one thing Astrid knew she could never compete with. For her own self-preservation, she had to end it, painful though it was.

Ultimately, she couldn't bear to be the other woman, her pride wouldn't stand for it.

There were no regrets. It was not Astrid's style. She had lived her life embracing every moment, every opportunity.

She returned to the letter, now finished, despite her throbbing head.

Best to check it over and read it out loud, something she always did when a letter was important.

"Oh, I must not forget to include the cheque."

She hoped to give the cheque to Amy at their next meeting, but just in case, she placed it in the envelope with the letter. The money was a drop in the ocean for Astrid, but a life changing sum for Amy.

She read the letter out loud, pausing occasionally to sip at her tea, and reflect on a word or sentence.

My dear Amy,
If you are reading this letter, it means that I have not been able to fulfil my intentions and meet you in person. I don't want my words and my actions to become lost in all the arrangements that are inevitable after a person dies.

I was not expected to live as long as I have, so writing this letter to you is a blessing, even though it does not feel like it at this precise moment.

I am so pleased that our paths crossed when they did, and that we have become friends.

I can't tell you how impressed I am with you Amy, and what a privilege it has been for me to pass on the lessons I have learned, after what feels like a lifetime in business, and of course to listen to your many amazing ideas. Your drive and enthusiasm are truly remarkable. I have seen you go the extra mile every time, with all the little things that I have asked you to do. This will undoubtedly stand you in good stead when you launch your business. Which you absolutely must!

I have so enjoyed our mentoring sessions, or rather 'conversations with a purpose' as I have always referred to them. Not to mention the scrumptious bakes that you have brought in for me. I have, on occasion, shared them with my boys, Steven and Mark. They have been unfailingly enthusiastic too. I confess that before writing this letter to you, I had the very last slice of your coffee and walnut cake. It was delicious! I have no doubt that you will profit from your passion, and profit you must, Amy. Don't let the grass grow under your feet!

I know from some of the things you have shared with me, that your upbringing was incredibly challenging, and that you have never been able to rely on either of your parents for support. Please don't let this hold you back. You are such a warm and engaging person that you will draw people to you, and some will want to help you just as I have.

Besides, you have more than enough talent and personality to succeed in life, and in business. Something I have told you many times over.

I know how hard it is to start a business, especially today when there is so much competition. To give you a head start, I have enclosed this gift. Steven said he would transfer it to your account if I could not hand it to you in person, but I still like good old-fashioned cheques when gifting money. So here it is! I don't have to tell you to spend it wisely, as I know you will. Having researched the going rental costs for retail units, I think this will more than cover them. However, if you negotiate a free first year of rent, you can then use this money for your start-up costs and marketing. Don't shrink from doing this!

In conclusion, I wish you so much happiness and success in the years that lie ahead, Amy. I might not be with you in person, but I hope you will be able to feel my presence. I only wish that we could have had more time together.

With love,

Astrid XX

Wiping the tears from her eyes, Astrid placed the letter carefully into its matching envelope, along with a cheque for £100,000.

It was the last letter and the last cheque she would ever write.

At the funeral, a single orchid with a sprig of forget-me-not arrived. The card had only one thing on it, one initial – the same initial on the back of Astrid's Cartier watch.

৵

Take love when
it comes
and rejoice.

Jodi Picoult

Chapter 6

Mary

Mary had conflicting feelings about arrangements for the day. On the one hand, she looked forward to spending it with Jess, her niece. On the other, she did not especially look forward to their visit to The Boutique.

Jess was, however, adamant about it.

They were going to find a wonderful new blouse for Mary. A departure from her usual safe choices. The invitation to a retirement party for an ex-colleague whom she held in high regard arrived, and Mary casually mentioned to Jess that she wasn't sure what to wear. Seizing on it, Jess suggested something new. She'd seen just the blouse, and today they were going to get it.

Mary immediately regretted mentioning the party to her niece.

And now they were both at The Boutique, Jess smiling at Jake, and Mary looking a little lost.

It was not Mary's usual type of clothes shop. It was so bright and big, with jazz music playing in the background. Diffusers and scented candles threw out all manner of exotic fragrance and tables festooned with jewellery, handbags, and boxes of glittery socks decorated every corner.

"Good morning, Jess, and who is this lovely lady with you today?"

Jake was on sparkling form, all smiles and warmth.

"Hi Jake. This lovely lady is my Aunty Mary and we're on a mission. She needs a very special new blouse for a retirement party she's going to. And it's tomorrow, so we have no time to waste!"

It was clear by Mary's demeanour that she did not want to spend any more time than was strictly necessary trying on blouses. It was fortuitous that Jake had been primed by Jess in an earlier phone call so could place the three blouses under consideration in the changing room. Jess had seen them online the night before, and despite Mary's misgivings, she was certain that one of them was just what Aunty Mary needed for the party.

"Please make yourself comfortable and ask if you need any help. I've hung up the three blouses in there."

Jake gestured to a spacious changing room that resembled an opulent Parisian boudoir. He hoped it would not drive Mary's senses into overload.

"Are you sure these are the blouses we looked at last night? They're much brighter than I recall."

Mary found her voice and looked at her niece, then back at Jake, a concerned expression on her face.

"Yes, they're the right ones...I think."

Jake looked at Jess for reassurance who nodded in agreement.

"If you look at the main colours in each blouse, Mary, they're subtle shades of cream, taupe, and caramel. These subtle extra touches, with the pastel colours of pink and lilac are designed to make each blouse look and feel more feminine and pretty. Try them on and let me know what you think. It's important that you're happy."

Jake's reassuring explanation had a positive impact on Mary, and she nodded her head, a faint smile playing on her face. After 15 minutes, Mary came out of the changing room behind Jess, to announce they had found 'the one', and that Jess would be buying it for her aunt as a belated birthday gift.

"Thank you for your help, Jake. I do believe it is a case of mission accomplished!"

"Yes, thank you, Jake. The blouse we settled on is just perfect for Aunty Mary's party tomorrow."

Jake was touched by Mary's acknowledgement of the minor part he had played in proceedings and pleased he had been able to help Jess.

Shopping trip completed; it was now time for a girls' lunch at their favourite restaurant. Something that Mary looked forward to after taking a walk on the wild side.

At the age of 16, Mary's life changed dramatically when her beloved mother, Isobel, died suddenly at the age of 42. Overnight, Mary became a mother to her four-year-old brother, Jack. She took over the running of the house and looked after her grieving father, John. As a stone mason of some repute, he worked long hours and could not shoulder any more responsibility.

Any thoughts Mary had of a career for herself had to be put to one side until Jack was old enough to look after himself. When Jack did reach 16, that magical age of independence, Mary, a 28-year-old single woman entered the working world, earning her own money for the first time in her life. Her very own wage-packet and the independence that went with it, was something she really appreciated. Having to ask her father for money for her personal use always made her uncomfortable, even though he did not begrudge her a penny. She had got used to getting by, and sometimes sacrificing her personal needs to avoid the awkwardness of asking.

That time had now passed, however, and there she was, earning a regular wage.

John, Mary's father wanted her to have every penny of her wage packet. It was the least he could do after the sacrifices she had made looking after him and Jack. Mary put some of the money to good use, making the bungalow more feminine and cosier, always keeping some to one side for the savings' account she had opened for Jack.

John was adamant that Mary should make up for lost time, and she did; she took several holidays abroad, but never exceeding a week to 10 days. She didn't want to leave her father or her brother for too long.

Mary was not a person to hold grudges or to be resentful about her life, and how different it would have been if her mother were still alive. Of course, she desperately missed her, But Mary belonged to a generation of women that just 'got on with it.' You would never hear her complain or lament the fact that her life could have been so much easier had she not had to shoulder so much responsibility at such an early age.

Besides, she loved her brother Jack and looked upon him as a son more than a sibling.

The feeling was mutual. Every Mother's Day, without fail, Mary received a beautiful bouquet of flowers, from Jack. He never missed, and over the years, the arrangements became quite spectacular, filling several vases. They did not come with a card, however. It wasn't necessary for Jack to convey his feelings or gratitude to Mary through words on paper. He adored her, and she was fully aware of that fact.

The only 'mother' Jack ever knew, was Mary, and in his eyes, she was the perfect mum.

When Mary started work, it was no surprise to anyone that she became a success. However, neither ambition nor a desire to reach the pinnacle of her profession as quickly as possible, motivated Mary. She was a meticulous and hard-working person, with endless amounts of patience. If there was a problem, she worked through it methodically and patiently until it was resolved. Given her job involved spreadsheets, tax calculations and managing budgets, it was a perfect marriage of talent meeting tasks. The hours were long and the work often challenging and thankless, but Mary never complained. She instilled the same ethos in her team.

Before she retired, Mary managed a team of 12. Her management style could best be described as minimal. If her staff were performing well, which they invariably were, and work was being completed accurately and on time, she didn't feel the need to micromanage. She would, however, happily allocate funds for training if any member of her team requested it, or she felt a person required additional support. But rousing team talks and team building away-days were not her strong suit. She preferred one-to-one conversations, and it seemed to work well for everyone.

Always caring and thoughtful in her nature, she never forgot a team member's birthday and brought in homemade cakes and biscuits on those occasions. Leading by example made her a popular boss.

As she prepared to wind-down and retire, she took to heart the responsibility of training her successor. Mary and David worked closely together for the nine months prior to her retirement. It was probably because David was elevated to her level of management that she allowed her guard down and they became friends.

Everyone had a deep fondness for Mary, and every member of her team spoke movingly about their unassuming, polite, and likeable manager at her retirement party.

When it came to relationships, true love had only come knocking on Mary's door once in her life. She formed a strong friendship with one man, William Ratcliffe, whom she had met on a walking holiday, with friends. Their courtship, as it would be described back then, consisted of trips to the opera and walks in the Yorkshire Dales. Theirs was a love that ended abruptly. William died unexpectedly, just two years after their first meeting. Mary grieved his loss in solitude, visiting his grave on the anniversary of his death, to lay flowers. She occasionally allowed herself to think again about what might have been.

Fun and irreverence came into Mary's life in the shape of her brother's two children, Jess, and Adam. The children struggled with their parents' divorce, so kind and patient Aunty Mary became the port in their storm. The two young children were immensely grateful for her calming and steadfast influence when their world spun too fast for them to keep up.

They both loved their aunt very much and as they grew older, involved her in every aspect of their lives.

Now, in the final chapters of her life, Mary accepted that she was and always would be a single woman. Love had only visited her once. She was quite sure it would not strike again. She thought it best not to dwell too much on it. Indulging her feelings was not something she ever allowed for herself. And besides, as she often told Jess and Adam, there were always people that were far worse off. You had to accept what life brought your way and make the best of it.

Back home in the peace and quiet of her bungalow, Mary had doubts about her new blouse. She steamed it, and placed it on a hanger, and was talking to herself, talking over her problems - as she had since the loss of her mother.

"It does seem flamboyant for my taste...I do like the sleeves and the neckline...I've never worn pink with taupe before...Am I too old for it? Oh, I'm just going to have to wear it and trust Jess."

'Flamboyant' was not a word that often featured in Mary's vocabulary.

And she was not a woman inclined to self-doubt. She made decisions in a careful and considered manner.

Better to be careful and address the pros and cons, than to be spontaneous and regret it afterwards. Nobody would describe Mary as reckless.

Mary was the introvert member of the family. She was the shy and reflective person at any gathering. She listened to what was being said and allowed the vocal people to dominate the conversation. She was always more than happy to blend into the background.

By contrast, Jess was the extrovert. Jess was the liveliest, most outgoing character of the family; always sharing what was on her mind, what she was thinking, where she was going. Jess made decisions quickly, underpinned by self-assuredness and confidence. In the time it had taken Mary to decide on the one blouse, Jess would have bought an entire outfit.

The blouse was not, by any stretch of the imagination, flamboyant.

It was simply a departure from Mary's usual, conservative tastes. If she was honest with herself, the departure had shaken her a little. Her taste in clothes had been challenged by her niece. And now, here she stood, with a blouse for which she felt no real enthusiasm.

But only Jess could do this to her.

She smiled, thinking about her niece, an inimitable whirlwind. Mary loved Jess dearly and could forgive her anything. And she understood why Jess encouraged her to be a touch more adventurous with her wardrobe. By her own admission, Mary was stuck in a rut, but it was nevertheless a rut she felt no pressing urge to escape!

The previous evening, Jess told Mary, in her customary blunt manner, that she was hiding herself in beige and grey or 'greige' as she described it. Her clothes were borderline frumpy. She played it safe, and it aged her. It was time to expand her colour palette and embrace some new patterns and colours. Nothing too dramatic, simply introducing a few pastel shades that would flatter her figure and her face.

But in this light, and compared to Mary's other blouses, her new blouse was too patterned and fussy for her liking.

She placed it carefully in the wardrobe, returning to the lounge to finish her crossword, muttering out loud.

"That's enough. I'm wearing it tomorrow. It'll be the first time and the last time, however."

Waking up the next day, Mary had reconsidered.

She took the blouse out of the wardrobe in the morning and could see it in an altogether more positive light. Perhaps it was the morning sun that softened the colours. Or was it just that having slept on it, she could see how cautious, even stubborn, she might have been the day before? It was most likely a combination of the two. She felt embarrassed about her behaviour toward Jess. Although most of her criticism about the blouse had taken place when she was alone, she still felt childish. She would ring Jess before she set off, to thank her for the blouse. It was such a thoughtful gift, bought with the best of intentions. That would give her time to catch the train and have a coffee in town before the retirement party.

The phone rang.

"Aunty Mary, are you ready to rock?"

Jess had beaten Mary to it.

"I hope you're wearing your gorgeous new blouse. No excuses, you looked stunning in it."

"Hello impish niece. Well, you'll be pleased with me, I've just put the blouse on."

Mary adjusted her necklace, a slender strand of pale pink freshwater pearls. It looked demure against the silky fabric of her blouse.

"And you may be right. I think the touch of pink does suit me quite nicely, and my pearls, the ones you bought me for my birthday, they look fetching with it."

"I'm feeling faint, Aunty Mary. Are you hinting that you may be open to more shopping trips with me? Trips to buy clothes for you, and not just for me?"

"Well, I wouldn't go quite that far. Let's see how today goes. It is a nice blouse. Certainly not something I would have picked myself. As you well know, niece!"

Jess laughed down the phone.

"No, if you'd chosen a blouse, it would be a tribute to greige. And like everything else you have in your wardrobe. 'The greige wardrobe'...now that would make a great title for a book. You could be the central character!"

Mary smiled.

"I'll let you know how I get on. And thank you for yesterday. I did enjoy it. Especially the lunch. We will pay a return visit soon."

"I'll be thinking of you. Go out there and rock your look, Aunty Mary. Show them what a sassy, sexy and smart retired woman you are. Don't forget to ring me afterwards."

Mary had no intention of being sassy or sexy.

Mary arrived in town an hour before the party, exactly as planned. Time to have a cup of coffee in her usual café and spend a few minutes checking her makeup – a touch of foundation, a smudge of blusher and a single sweep of lipstick. As Jake had indeed said, the blouse was pretty, and she did feel happy to wear it, much better in daylight than in the full glare of the changing room lights. It complemented her jacket and matching skirt. Another outfit she had bought under Jess's watchful eye.

She couldn't remember when she had last worn an outfit so noticeable, and at the same time, so smart and eye-catching. But everything felt fine and, fitted; no tightness, nothing gaping. Jess was right. She would make a point of listening to her more often, when the subject of fashion for the older woman reared its head.

At ten minutes to three, she entered The Smiling Duck, frowning slightly at the sign and the wording.

What a silly name for a wine bar. Why do people have to assign behaviours to animals or birds that are quite clearly inaccurate?

"Mary! Over here. Come and join us!"

She recognised the voice, and for a moment was confused. Had she got the time wrong? She'd checked the invitation a few times and it most definitely said 3pm. She saw a table full of some ex-colleagues and her heart sank. Most at that table were clearly intoxicated. She did not relish the thought of joining them to answer ridiculous drink-fuelled questions. Thankfully, another group she recognised stood chatting by the bar. They didn't appear to be under the influence of alcohol. She decided to join that group, edging her way past the small tables that spilled over with noisy people, clearly in good spirits, making an early start to the weekend.

She had already decided to excuse herself after an hour. She could wait for her taxi in the café next door.

"Mary, how are you? You look amazing. That colour suits you so well."

Linda, from accounts gave her a surprise hug. Not one for exuberance with anyone, let alone ex-colleagues, Mary nevertheless responded by tapping Linda gently on the back.

"Thank you. Am I late? I thought the retirement party started at 3pm."

Mary glanced nervously at her watch.

"No, you're right, Mary. We were allowed off work half an hour earlier."

Malcolm, one of the managers from accounts smiled at her.

"Retirement suits you, Mary. You look very well."

"Thank you. I'm keeping myself busy. I hope you're well."

Mary remained at a loss for what else to say to him, and for that matter, to anyone. When she worked with those people, it didn't matter that she was the quiet one in the office. She could hide behind the fact that she was their manager. Besides, they all knew she was not one for small talk.

However, after half an hour spent mostly listening to other people, whilst sipping slowly on a glass of white wine, Mary began to relax and was able to join in with some of the conversations. Two small glasses of wine were her absolute limit though, and there was no talking her out of that, despite the many offers to buy her a drink.

Mary was aware that she had not yet spoken to David. It was his retirement party. He kept looking over and smiling, but they were both caught up in conversations that neither could leave without appearing rude. She hoped they would find time to catch up before the party ended, but her taxi was due in 30 minutes.

Time was running out.

Feeling overwhelmed by the noise and the gathering pace of the drinking, Mary made an excuse to 'powder her nose.'

She was pleasantly surprised to see David approaching her as she emerged from the cloakroom.

"Mary, I am so pleased to see you at last; thank you for coming. I've been wanting to catch up with you since you walked in."

He beckoned her to an empty table with two armchairs.

"Let's sit here, so we can talk in peace. It's so noisy in there."

The table was like an oasis for Mary, she never felt at ease standing at a bar. She was really pleased to see

David, and relieved with his suggestion of a catch up in this relatively tranquil space. There was still time for conversation before her taxi arrived.

They sat facing each other until David spoke, breaking their few seconds of silence.

"You look very well, Mary, and your outfit is so smart. How's your retirement suiting you? I'm aware that we haven't spoken since you left, and I've really wanted to catch up with you, on more than one occasion in the last year."

David looked at her intently. He noticed that she blushed.

"Thank you. I have my niece to thank for my outfit..."

Mary's voice trailed off. She suddenly found it hard to speak to David with any degree of confidence or certainty. Her words were somewhere, albeit buried deep inside her, struggling to reach the surface. After what seemed like an eternity, she managed to respond to his question.

"Well...retirement is certainly different to working, and there are some rewarding aspects to it. I'm keeping busy as a volunteer at a local charity for the homeless, and I enjoy spending time with my niece and nephew. When they're not working, that is. And how about you, David? Are you looking forward to your retirement? I thought you had longer to go than just a year."

Mary always preferred to be the one asking questions than talking about herself.

She studied David closely whilst waiting for his answer. She thought he looked well. He was still trim, and his dress sense was, as ever, impeccable. She always thought he had the nicest smile of any man she had ever met, and his eyes were a bright, piercing blue. He had always been so courteous and chivalrous. How kind of him to notice her outfit. Why had he wanted to contact her over the last year? Why did he want to talk to her now, away from the main party? Had his eyes always sparkled like that?

All those thoughts swirled around in Mary's head. She could feel her heart pounding in her chest. What on earth was happening to her?

Eventually, David spoke.

"I'm looking forward to my early retirement very much, Mary. And I'm hoping to go to the theatre and the opera more often."

He smiled at Mary again, then he reached over to hold her hand.

Mary felt light-headed. Was it the wine, or was it her nerves that were the cause of her rapidly accelerating heartbeat and the sudden feeling of dizziness?

The last time she had felt like this was, well…it was many years ago.

Still holding her hand, David cleared his throat.

"In fact, Mary, I hoped that you and I could go to the theatre. I remember you saying you liked the opera. I happen to have two tickets for Tosca at the Royal Opera House in three weeks' time. I would love to take you as my guest. Is that something that appeals to you?"

Mary could scarcely believe her ears.

The response came tumbling out of her mouth before she could even think about it.

"That sounds nice, David."

David smiled inwardly at Mary's understated response. She had not changed in the past year. She was still the same sweet and modest Mary.

"I'm so pleased you would, Mary. And perhaps we could go on some lovely walks later in the year? If we enjoy each other's company at the opera, that is. It's much better to stride out with a good friend than it is to walk alone, wouldn't you agree?"

Mary tried to take everything in. What David said felt...so natural. Simply marvellous, in fact. Jess and Adam would be thrilled with her news. They were always telling her to get out more, to live life to the full, to really enjoy herself after a lifetime of putting everybody else first.

It was time for her to push out of her comfort zone again. Twice in two days!

"I would like that very much, David. So yes, please, to the opera and yes to the lovely walks."

Taking a deep breath to steady her nerves, she patted his hand.

Another visit to The Boutique may be in order. I did see a few discreet gowns in pastel tones that would be just the ticket for the opera. Maybe Jess would like to come shopping again...

David beamed at Mary, squeezing her hand, over the moon with her response; grateful that at long last, he had summoned enough courage speak to her in this manner. How he had waited for this moment, rehearsing what he was going to say to her over and over, anticipating rejection, but hoping she would say yes. And she had. He couldn't believe his ears, either. He wasn't going to let Mary slip through his fingers.

I am so delighted that you have accepted my invitation to the opera, Mary, because I want you to know that I love you and I have loved you for many years. I hope that in time you will also come to love me, but we can go at your pace. Hopefully we have the rest of our lives together.

He didn't say this to her, of course.

One day...

෨

Chapter 7

Caroline

Caroline revelled in a positive frame of mind. 'That's twice in as many months.' She thought. Today's errand, to collect her interview outfit from The Boutique, a sumptuous velvet trouser suit in the softest shade of lilac, with colour matching buttons gave her a boost. It had only been in the window for a few hours when she saw it and immediately declared it hers. The single-breasted jacket, with satin lapels accentuated her curves, while the trousers fitted beautifully, albeit a few inches longer than the desired length. Jake arranged a tailor to take them up in record breaking time. The improbable task accomplished, trousers altered to the perfect length and delivered back to The Boutique - within 24 hours of Caroline trying the suit on for the first time.

She, as usual, left everything to the last minute.

She also hoped to find a bag to match the suit, to hold samples of work she needed to take to the interview. The beloved-but-battered tote bag, her constant companion since Uni, no longer cut a dazzling first impression. It looked unkempt against the backdrop of the striking trouser suit. And now she was unsure about the t-shirt she planned to wear.

Some last-minute inspiration from Jake was required. Walking into The Boutique for the second time in two days, Caroline felt relaxed and confident about her impending interview. Four hours to go, with the clock ticking. After the past year, she was determined that today of all days, she was not going to allow herself to be consumed by irrational fears and unbridled sadness. There was plenty of time to finalise her entire outfit, change into it, travel into London and stop for a coffee at the station.

The white t-shirt she originally planned to wear was stuffed unceremoniously into the shabby tote bag, just in case she couldn't find an alternative.

"Hi Jake, I'm back, but I'm not keen on the t-shirt anymore. I'm fancying something like...this."

She pointed at the jade green t-shirt on one of the mannequins.

"Hopefully, you have it in my size. It stands out more than plain old white, and besides, it's much more me."

"Hi Caroline, how wonderful to see you again, your suit was delivered an hour ago."

Jake pointed to the trouser suit hanging on the rail at the back of the till area, protected by a transparent suit cover.

"The trousers are the right length. I've measured them. And I agree, this t-shirt has more drama. It only came in this morning."

He removed it carefully from the mannequin.

"This size should fit you, and the colour palette is just perfect, Jade green with lilac. A glorious combination, especially for a creative person. Would you like to try everything on, and have a final inspection of your gorgeousness in the mirror?"

"Perfect, Jake, thank you."

Caroline headed for the changing room.

"And I don't know if you clocked it, but I have the same shade of green in my trainers. I just need a bag now, so I'm hoping you can rustle up something that will pull all the pieces together."

She popped her head around the changing room curtain.

"Tell me you have!"   149

Jake was used to Caroline leaving everything to the last minute. Thankfully, he had just the bag for her.

"What do you think of this? It has your name all over it."

He handed her a faux leather tote bag - a fusion of the colours in her outfit and trainers. It was also big enough to accommodate all her work.

"I love it all Jake. The bag, the t-shirt, the trouser suit...they're all simply perfect."

Caroline's voice wavered.

"Part of me is so happy, and the other part feels bereft and heartbroken...I'm sorry."

She began to cry.

"I hate the feeling of being on top of the world one minute and wanting to hide from everybody the next. Grief is just..."

She emerged from the changing room like a lost soul.

"...so consuming and draining. Nothing prepared me for this."

Jake looked at her sympathetically.

"I know Caroline, everything is still so raw for you. You're bound to feel like this. I don't want to talk in cliches, but your dad would be so proud of you. And you will look beautiful. You're going to wow them at the interview. So, try to hold it together for the next few hours, until the job offer is in the bag, pardon the pun. There'll be time afterwards to become a puddle."

"Thank you. Better to get the tears out of the way now, I guess."

She wiped her eyes using the tissue Jake handed to her.

"I love everything, so can you give me a few minutes? I'll smarten up and transfer all my work from this specimen..."

She held up the tatty tote bag.

"...to this thing of beauty."

Caroline knew that she would not be going for a second interview if her dad, Alan, was still alive. Four months since his death, might as well have been yesterday. Her emotions were still so raw.

She missed him dreadfully. The finality of his death had not yet fully surfaced – like a deep bruise, until it developed completely, the healing couldn't begin properly. She wasn't sure if she ever would heal. In moments of sorrow, of which there were many, she found herself envying those with a firm religious faith. They believed they would see their loved ones again. What comfort. If only she could believe that too.

After paying for the alterations and thanking Jake profusely, Caroline made her way to the station, hoping that after today, she would be starting a fresh chapter in her life.

Before Caroline's dad was diagnosed with inoperable pancreatic cancer, she had been a successful graphic designer for a local firm, winning several awards for her work. It was a career she loved. But after his diagnosis, she handed in her notice and moved in with him so they could be together in his final months. She had always been close to him. Theirs was an incredibly warm and loving relationship, made even more special and intense because Caroline's mum died when she was only 10.

So, for Caroline, there was no question that she would be with her dad at the end of his life. She could think of nothing more important.

For the first two months, they were inseparable. In between chemotherapy sessions, her dad wanted to tick off everything on his small, but perfectly curated bucket list. Nothing spectacular such as skydiving from planes or swimming with dolphins, he simply wanted to return to the places where they'd holidayed together, when Caroline was a little girl. They had several days out to the seaside towns on his list, visiting favourite restaurants and cafés. They even went on a few boat excursions, although one made him feel quite unwell. They both remembered the boat trips being longer, and the queues so much shorter back then.

In the evenings, when Caroline was in bed, she finally allowed herself to dwell on what was round the corner. Her heart filled with sorrow, and desperation addled her mind, terrifying her with thoughts of losing him. Part of her mind refused to believe that he was really dying. Dad made sure he was there for every event, no matter how small, just to make up for Caroline's mum leaving her. Every birthday, Christmas concert, sports day, award ceremony, he missed nothing, not one precious moment. She never doubted he would be there for every landmark event in her life and looked forward to all the new highlights – marriage, children – she knew he would be the best granddad ever. Yet here she was, on the verge of becoming an orphan, with no future events for him to share with her.

Alan could see how much she struggled and although he tried to comfort her, it would often have the opposite effect. He too had to manage his emotions, overwhelming and unfathomable ones. So, on some days, they wore a mask of happiness to conceal their profound sadness. On other occasions, they managed to enjoy the day for what it was; a father and his daughter making memories, and enjoying each other's company, knowing that time was running out.

After a few months, with the bucket list nearing completion, Alan's health began to decline at an alarming rate. Plans for an occasional day out, a short walk, or an outing to a local café were made, only to be broken. Caroline tried tending to him for a few weeks, but it all became too much for them both. She felt woefully inadequate. When he tried to talk to her about his Will, she refused to listen. He tried to broach the subject of his new car; how he wanted his closest friend to have it, she broke down and couldn't stop crying. Why was he being so pessimistic? He may well live longer than the original diagnosis, so why was he talking to her about such morbid, unthinkable things?

Expert help and compassion came in the form of the Macmillan Nurses who took over from Caroline, then she harboured feelings of guilt for being relieved about it. But Alan was able to talk freely to the nurses about his last wishes, and it was far easier for Caroline to listen to the nurses than it was her dad. He spent the last week of his life in a local hospice, with Caroline by his side until he died.

In the early months after his death, Caroline was inconsolable, consumed by grief, barely able to subsist. The thought of returning to work frightened her, but the reality of waking up every morning with only her thoughts to keep her company frightened her more. She had to return to work for her own sanity, in the career she loved, but with a new company.

And now here she was, so close to getting that new job, with a company she had really taken a shine to, and the feeling seemed mutual. All the signs pointed to an offer being made. The first interview had been an informal chat, online, and she enjoyed it! It was lovely to talk about work again, and to receive really good feedback about her ideas and her experience. She was then asked to design a poster for the company. She agonised over the project, spending far too much time on something that, 12 months earlier, she would have completed in a few hours. Again, the feedback was positive, though.

The final stage, today's interview, was with one of the company partners who had been very complimentary about her work. All she had to do was keep her cool and talk him through her portfolio.

She could do that!

Caroline managed to find two seats to herself on the train. Quiet time to window gaze and take a last glance over the samples of work she had brought, collated in precise order inside the stylish new tote. She adored the tote bag. It was a glamorous but functional piece. The velvet suit felt so luxurious against her skin. She was thankful that she had decided on the jade green t-shirt. For the first time in months, she felt hopeful about her chances at the interview. She'd made it to the final two, but something told her she would be offered the job today. She felt as though her dad was with her, guiding her every move.

She was thrilled with her hair too - glossy and sleek perfection, all kinks and frizz blow-dried away by Lucia, her friend and hairdresser. Caroline's makeup, although subtle, accentuated her hazel eyes and brought a sun-kissed glow to her cheeks. It was the first time she had worn makeup since before her dad's death. The thought of that made her well up again. Time for distraction, looking at her work. Again.

And then came the delay.

There was no explanation why the train stopped abruptly between two stations. Nothing for 30 minutes, other than a pre-recorded statement that gave no specific information about the current predicament.

Caroline fought the urge to run when the train eventually pulled into London 40 minutes late. She allowed a calm voice of reason to prevail; the one she had been cultivating for the past week. She would still arrive at the office with 15 minutes to spare. There was no need to rush. The coffee would have to wait until after the interview, but that was no big deal.

The platform teemed with people rushing in all directions, talking intently into mobile phones, shouting at the platform staff about connecting trains. Every flurry of activity contributed to overwhelming chaos. Despite it all, Caroline remained unruffled, focussing on the interview and the questions she was likely to be asked. She held onto her new bag tightly. There was no way her new treasure, with all its precious contents was going anywhere other than to that interview.

Then, as if in slow motion...

The man in front of her tripped and landed in a crumpled heap on the floor, narrowly missing one of the concrete pillars. The contents of his satchel – mobile phone, a newspaper, a thick folder, and his lunch-box scattered in every direction. And still the people in front of and behind him kept on walking, as though nothing had happened. Some showed irritation at the sheer inconvenience of having to step around him. The platform staff seemed oblivious to any of it.

Caroline's first instinct was to do what everyone else did. Ignore. Walk on. Pretend it never happened. He'd be okay. She managed that for all of 20 seconds. Her mind began to race, two competing voices vying for attention.

"Continue. Don't look back. He'll be fine. I can't stop. I'll be late."

The other voice was, however, in complete opposition.

"I can't leave him. What if he's hurt? How would I feel in his shoes? What would Dad think of me? What if it had happened to Dad?"

Like a slap to the face, the last question hit her hard. She turned around.

Kneeling in front of the man sitting on the floor, looking dazed, she placed her hand gently on his shoulder.

"Hi, that looked like a nasty fall. Are you okay? Can I get you any help?"

She gazed at the floor. In amongst the rushing feet, she could see some of his possessions.

"Let me get your things. I don't think anything's broken."

She began picking up the contents of his bag, one item at a time, navigating around the oncoming feet. She handed over his bag and held firmly onto hers. There was no way she was going to lose her own bag at the expense of saving the contents of his.

"That is so kind of you, thank you."

The man regained his composure. He didn't look as though he had been badly hurt, just a bit shaken.

"I think I've bruised my ego more than anything but thank you for stopping to see if I was okay. And for finding all my stuff, I think you've recovered everything. You're the only person that cared enough to check on me. You see the best and the worst of human nature in these situations, don't you?"

Caroline held out her hand to help him to his feet.

"That's okay. Good news, there's no damage done."

They both smiled awkwardly.

She glanced at her watch. She could still make the interview, with five minutes to spare, if she hurried.

"Anyway, I must go now. I have a job interview, and I don't want to be late."

The man offered her his hand, which she took. To the outside world, it looked unusual; two strangers shaking hands in the middle of a busy platform. To Caroline, it felt as though it was absolutely the right thing to do.

The man smiled at her.

"Thank you again. I must ask your name. You've been so...well you've been amazing, really. And I can't tell you how grateful I am that you saved these. I'd be lost without them, especially the folder, and my phone."

"Oh, and good luck with your job interview."

"My name? Oh, it's Caroline...Caroline Edwards. Well, I'm pleased that you're okay and I'm glad I helped. Take care. Bye."

She couldn't spend a moment longer with him, because time was no longer on her side. Conscious that she had been kneeling on the floor, she made a beeline for the toilets on the concourse. A swift touch-up was required before heading to the office and the interview.

She would be five minutes late at the most, but hopefully they would be sympathetic towards her if she explained her reasons.

It was only when she looked at herself in the full-length mirror that she saw the extent of the damage. Two large, dirty marks on her trousers. On both knees, clearly from when she had been kneeling. And a dark, ugly looking smear on one of the pockets on her jacket. How on earth had that got there? Was it when they shook hands? Were his hands dirty from the fall? Regardless of its origin, there it was, joining the others, a hat-trick of stains.

Her heart sank.

15 minutes later, with two damp patches on her trousers after trying to remove the stains with water, soap, and paper-towels, Caroline arrived at her destination. She had given up trying to get rid of the stain on her jacket. The water made it look even darker. Hopefully, they would be looking at her face,

and of course, her portfolio more than her clothes. What a waste of a brand-new trouser suit. A good dry clean might restore it, but that was something to contemplate at another time.

She stood a million miles away from feeling optimistic about her chances. Her confidence levels plummeted. Because, to add to the ignominy of the entire debacle, her glossy, sleek hair, all shine and shimmer a few hours ago, had reverted to its naturally frizzy state. It stuck out in all directions, thanks to the light drizzle that started within minutes of walking out of the station. Of course she had not thought to bring an umbrella with her. She'd not checked on the weather forecast, her mind preoccupied with other, more important matters.

She didn't know whether to laugh, cry or to scream at the top of her voice.

Such dreadful bad luck. I look as though I've been dragged through a hedge backwards. Come on Dad. If you're there, now is the time to help me, because I'm going to need it, big time.

Arriving at her interview a full 20 minutes late, she was greeted by Claire who had interviewed her previously. A friendly woman, she appeared sympathetic to Caroline's clearly dishevelled appearance, especially when she heard the reason for her lateness. Thankfully, Lance Rogers, the partner interviewing her was in a meeting, so Caroline was invited to sit in the staff restaurant. She declined the offer of a fresh coffee, tempting though it sounded. Given the circumstances, she would have welcomed several shots of caffeine, but instead chose the safer option of water. At least if that landed on her trousers, it wouldn't cause a stain.

She looked down at her trouser suit and shook her head.

All that money, all that effort to create a knock-out look and for what? The only redeeming feature was the t-shirt. If it had any stains, they were not visible. She shuddered. Being a good Samaritan had cost her dear. Sipping the water, she tried to reset her mind by repeating affirmations under her breath.

Thirty minutes later, Claire returned and took Caroline to a meeting room at the end of a long corridor. Caroline knocked, already removing the samples of work from her bag.

A man in his early forties stood up from behind his desk and moved forward to introduce himself, Lance Rogers, partner at the firm.

Caroline could feel her adrenaline pumping. The room was quite dark, so the stains on her trouser suit would not show up so much, she hoped. She was keen to get started, to put the last few hours firmly behind her.

Before she could open her mouth, he stopped her in her tracks.

"Now I'm not sure if you are aware, Caroline, for this job, you were one of two candidates who reached the final stage. I was hoping to interview you both together, before making the final decision. Claire has explained the reason why you were unable to make the interview on time, and I fully understand. However, the other candidate really stood out and is an exceptionally good fit for our company and our values. So, we've decided to offer her the job.

I understand how disappointing this must be for you, and I'm sorry you've had a wasted trip. We will of course, reimburse your expenses if you leave your details with Claire on your way out."

Caroline was oblivious to anything further he might have said after mentioning Claire's name. Her mind reeled from the blow he delivered. She was vaguely aware of shaking his hand before being ushered politely out of the room. Then she rushed back through the corridor, down two floors in the lift, and into the fresh air. Expenses could wait for another day.

She didn't want to spend another moment in that wretched building.

Any effort to compose herself failed miserably; tears streamed down her cheeks. More tears to add to the thousands she had cried in the last year, but for a different reason.

This is so unfair. That stupid, clumsy man at the station has ruined everything. Why didn't I just leave him to sort himself out, like everyone else? I would have made it to the interview on time, and I'm sure I would've got the job. So much for helping a stranger out. I'm never doing that again. And who on earth offers a job to someone straight after their interview, whilst another person is waiting to go in? That's hardly a level playing field. What a demeaning experience, and a brutal punishment for being kind to a stranger. Karma was not on my side today. Back to square one. And my trouser suit is probably ruined.

On the train home, and with a long-awaited cup of coffee cradled in her hands, Caroline went over the previous few hours. She settled into a more reflective mood; the shock of being told she had not got the job receded into the distance. She looked down at her trouser suit yet again, shaking her head and sighing loudly enough for a few of the passengers to glance over at her, before promptly returning to their mobile phones.

Would I change what I did earlier to help that man? Probably not. Dad has always taught me to be compassionate and helpful when people are in trouble, not to ignore them. Besides, karma doesn't have to be repaid on the very same day of a good deed. And I know that I'm ready to start working again. It's not the end of the world, being passed over for this job. What a miserable lot. They chose to reject me because I was late for a good reason. If they can't see a talented and decent person when one is offered up to them, it's their loss. I don't want to work for a company like that. And I won't be calling them again. I'm not bothered about listening to their reasons why the other candidate was such a perfect fit for them and their values. Stuff that. Stuff them. I'll cover my own expenses rather than grovel to them, and I'll just chalk it all down to experience.

Yep! I'd do the same thing again tomorrow, and I know Dad would be proud of me, prouder of me for helping that man than ignoring him and getting the job. There'll be other jobs...better jobs, and there'll be other trouser suits. I reckon I've done good today.

"Thank you, Dad."

Chapter 8

Sophie

You didn't want to get on the wrong side of Sophie.

You'd get away with a ticking off for unreasonable or unfair behaviour, but the big stuff – deception, lying and bullying - she was fearless in those situations, even if it meant compromising on her own safety, or jeopardising her position.

Today was going to be a day like no other for her; she had thought long and hard about it all for some time. What she needed to say, who would be involved, and the ripple effect of her actions. She felt invincible, knowing that it didn't matter one iota how people reacted. Right was unequivocally on her side.

She needed to be resolute in her mission. And heads, or rather one head, would roll.

But before she could put her plans into action, Sophie had more practical things to do. She had to collect a bag from The Boutique for her sister, Jane's, birthday. An oversized black and white crossbody bag in her favourite style; the thing she had pointed out to Sophie when asked what she wanted for her birthday.

The Boutique was not really Sophie's type of shop when she went looking for clothes and accessories. Purely a jeans and plain t-shirts girl, with denim jackets and scant jewellery, shopping trips were tedious for Sophie. Designer trainers and boots were her only indulgence. She wore her late father's wedding ring on her right hand, with a vintage watch from her grandmother. A slender gold chain, a gift from her mother completed her entire jewellery wardrobe. She was a woman firmly on the minimal side of the spectrum, regardless of the occasion. But she invariably made her way to The Boutique when buying presents, realising that the clothes and accessories to be found there were ideal gifts for many of her friends and family.

In the past year, Sophie had got to know Kelly and had grown to like her. What Kelly had accomplished for her business, without the slightest hint of support, was something quite special to say the least. And Kelly was such an unassuming and modest person. Sophie noticed that whereas others would talk at length about their bold plans, Kelly got on with hers without making a fuss.

And the results were astonishing, from a market stall to a thriving business with a large online shop, and a significant social following. Similarly, Kelly always appeared pleased to see Sophie, eager to find out more about what was happening at the theatre, and how seats were selling for their latest production. She admired Sophie's confident and forthright manner.

"Good morning, Sophie. How lovely to see you. Twice in three days!"

The two women had seen each other at a networking event earlier in the week, where Kelly had been the guest speaker.

"It's lovely to see you too, Kelly. I really enjoyed the meeting, and I thought your talk was inspiring. You should do more public speaking. Now, I'm here to collect the bag I ordered online yesterday. I thought I'd take advantage of the time I have on my hands before starting work."

Kelly was pleased to hear such positive feedback on her talk, especially from Sophie. She was not one to give throwaway compliments, so when she did say something positive, she really meant it.

"I enjoyed the meeting too, even though I was in the hot seat. I'm starting to get used to public speaking, but don't quote me on that! Next week, I'm speaking at The Business Show in London, of all places, so I really must up my game. I've half a mind to cancel it, because the thought of speaking to a massive audience, using a microphone, terrifies me...but it's such a powerful way to promote the business. And I'm a last-minute stand-in, due to a cancellation, so it would look bad if I called it off now, I guess. And you're right. Public speaking is something I should do more of. I've got to put my negative thoughts to one side and jump in!"

Kelly smiled and shuddered at the same time. She'd not had chance to fully process the fact that, within days, she'd be standing on a stage, narrating her business success story to hundreds of strangers. Best to stop thinking about it, for now. Back to the present moment and the safe space of her shop.

"I've wrapped the bag, because as I recall from your message, it's for a birthday gift. I hope you approve. Yesterday, I had one customer tell me they would rather Jake did the honours. I didn't take it personally. Not one bit."

Pulling a face of mock dismay, Kelly handed the bag to Sophie.

"It looks lovely, Kelly. No complaints from me. And The Business Show? Now that is some event to speak at. Good on you. Don't cancel it! And I must say, I am loving that dress on you. Wear something like that next week, and you'll have the whole audience on your website, putting in orders!"

Kelly wore a red printed dress with a vibrant pattern, comprising tigers, palm trees and toucans. Her hair was loosely fastened at the back with a two large, red, silk poppies, masquerading as hair clips. As usual, she appeared effortlessly stylish and stunning.

"Oh, I'm glad you approve. This is a new line of Fairtrade dresses we're introducing over the next month. I'm just testing the water with customers, and so far, the reaction has been great. This dress also comes in pale blue. Not quite as stand-out, but just as stunning and..."

Kelly paused for the kill.

"... you know, Sophie, I reckon you'd look lovely in the blue one. Why don't you try it on?"

Sophie smiled, shaking her head. Kelly was undoubtedly modest about her achievements in business, but she was an accomplished hustler, always looking for the next sale.

And she was so good at promoting the clothes in The Boutique - the ultimate ambassador for her brand.

"As you know, dresses are not my thing, but these are."

Sophie held up a pair of cowboy boots in an opulent chocolate, faux suede material.

"What a colour. It's such a rich shade, and they'll look great with my jeans. If you have them in a size six, I'll take them now."

"I do, and I'm so glad you like them!"

Kelly was pleased with the unexpected additional sale from Sophie.

"These are the last pair in your size. The stock only came in yesterday, and already we're down to single figures. Are you sure you don't want to try them on?"

She handed Sophie the boots in their box.

"No. I don't really have the time, but I'm sure they'll fit. Thank you again for wrapping the bag for me. And before I forget, good luck for next week. The audience are in for a treat!"

The twenty-minute drive to work gave Sophie enough time to focus on what she was going to say, and how she would react if things turned nasty. She'd run through every probable scenario many times over, making notes so she could refine certain points. She checked and checked again that she still had the recording, and the copy. She was determined to go in fully prepared. She would not allow her nerves to get the better of her or lose control of the situation. There was no chance of that happening today.

Work had not always been fraught with drama for Sophie. After leaving school with a handful of qualifications, she spent several years travelling around the world. She took on various jobs: waitressing, cleaning, child-minding - earning enough money to pay for the next stage of her adventure.

Returning home, her focus was on finding a career that could hold her interest. After a few months of searching, she struck gold and was offered a position as PR manager for a local theatre. It was clear to the people interviewing, that what she lacked in experience, she more than made up for in attitude and character.

The role proved to be satisfying, if demanding.

Anti-social hours were the norm, as was the need to massage the egos of some performers, which she found testing. The smaller the star, the bigger the ego, but Sophie accepted it as being part of the job.

Eventually, after working long hours for more than two years, without so much as an entire week off, Sophie issued her boss, Alex, with an ultimatum. They either find the money for the promised assistant to support her, or she would leave. Alex knew she wasn't one for making empty promises, so the funds miraculously appeared, and Maggy joined Sophie's team as her capable and competent assistant.

Everyone in the theatre liked and respected Sophie, not least because she always managed to get the best out of people. She was a diligent worker, and unfailingly honest. Colleagues knew where they stood and could count on her support if they needed help or were out of their depth. Although her official role was as head of PR, Alex increasingly looked upon Sophie as his right-hand person, someone he could trust implicitly, and rely upon for an honest opinion on any matter to do with the theatre. Sophie was, for her part, happy with the situation at work. She saw opportunities for growth, she loved mentoring Maggy, and she enjoyed working with Alex. He was a decent man and an equally decent boss.

Everything ticked along nicely until James joined as the new sales manager.

By invitation, Sophie attended James' second interview, along with the head of HR.

She had reservations about him.

James offered an undoubtedly impressive CV. On paper, he possessed every quality they asked for, including wide-ranging experience gained from working with other theatres. And he certainly had a good track record based on the sales figures he quoted.

He appeared engaging and self-assured; undeniably important qualities for the role, but towards the end of the interview, he started to flirt a little with both women, becoming overly familiar in the process. Nothing too obvious, or crass, but it nevertheless made Sophie question the real character that lurked beneath the otherwise polished performance.

That kind of behaviour might have been acceptable years ago, but times had moved on. Why hadn't he? Sophie decided not to say anything about her misgivings to Alex. Other than James' lack of propriety, he came across well and filling the role quickly seemed a priority for the theatre.

Time was not on their side. Besides, it was unlikely she would spend too much time working with James. The initial projects that were lined up for him would not impact on her work. He had his own office, so their paths would not often cross.

For the first year, the doubts Sophie gleaned from the interview seemed unfounded. They rarely came into direct contact with one another, and on the odd occasions when they did, James behaved in a respectful and polite manner. No more red flags. They even managed to work well together on a project which required both their skill sets in equal measure.

Sophie found James quite funny at the end of year work's party. The flirtatious nature on display in the interview was thankfully conspicuous by its absence. He seemed good fun, easy going, even charming. In the months after the work's party, he continued in the same vein, pleasant and professional. However, Sophie still chose to keep her distance.

There was something about him that she didn't like, or more to the point, didn't trust. But she couldn't quite put her finger on it.

Soon the feeling of unease grew. Sophie began to see signs that James concentrated on nothing more than furthering his career at all costs.

It was when she overheard him talking to a journalist, casually claiming that he was the driving force behind a new show selling out, that she finally saw his untrustworthy, self-serving nature. They had both worked on the project, with a shared responsibility to give it as much promotion as possible. Yet there he was, erasing her efforts, cutting her from it, claiming it was his magic touch, and his alone that filled the seats for the sold-out five-night performance.

When Sophie challenged James about the overheard conversation, he became defensive and agitated. James claimed that had she continued to eavesdrop on his private conversation, she would have heard him tell the journalist, in some detail, about her role in the project. He accused Sophie of being paranoid, and she should, in future, stay away from him.

Convinced he was lying; Sophie could prove nothing.

Little by little, James' mask began to slip, to reveal his true nature.

Sophie became suspicious of his intentions when he started to cosy up to Alex, joining him on the occasional vape break to start with. James didn't vape, so to Sophie, his reasons were obvious.

He was trying to wheedle his way into Alex's good books.

She hoped Alex would see it too, but she didn't feel it was her place to broach the subject.

Yet.

James would surely expose himself at some stage. As she observed, people like him inevitably became over-confident and overplayed their hand. She bided her time.

Things came to a head sooner than she could have anticipated.

Alex left the theatre without notice. One day he was at his desk, the next, he had quit. Three days later, James was announced as Alex's successor.

None of it made any sense to Sophie. Why would Alex just up and leave without saying anything to members of the team? Granted, there had clearly been something troubling him in the week up to his departure. She'd put it down to the time of year. He worked ridiculously hard on finalising the programme for the following year, but surely that was not the reason why.

Sophie was not only perplexed, she was hurt, too.

James' skill set lay a million miles away from making him a natural heir apparent. He had neither the experience nor the talent to fill Alex's boots. Why had he been the only contender for the role? Why had she not been considered? Sophie would have declined the role if it had been offered to her, but to be passed over in favour of a colleague who clearly lacked skills in so many areas, made no sense whatsoever.

Around then, Sophie decided she no longer wanted to work at the theatre. It was time for a new challenge, time for something she'd been thinking about and working on for several months.

Before taking the final step, she needed to dig deeper into the reasons behind Alex's departure, and ultimately, James' stratospheric rise to his position. What she discovered shocked her to the core, but at the same time, once she processed everything, it did not surprise her in the least.

And she decided today was going to be the day of reckoning for James. He thought he had got away with everything, but Sophie wanted him to be without doubt of the fact that he had not, not by the longest of chalks.

Whatever else happened, by the end of the working day, Sophie intended the events would force a massive shake-up in the theatre. She decided to go out with a bang, taking James out with her – either by his resignation or by scandal and ruination of his entire future career in theatre.

One thing she had learned in her varied career, 'Go big or go home' got everyone's attention.

Driving into the car park, she checked James' car was parked in his designated place, his name newly etched on the metal plate. He'd wasted no time in getting that done, she observed with a wry smile.

The first piece of the plan was in place: make sure the target is present.

"Afternoon Sophie, how's things? Busy day?"

Sophie smiled at Tony, the theatre's caretaker. He looked up from the task of removing every piece of litter from the car park in his customary, meticulous manner to speak to her.

"Hi Tony. Great as always. You're doing a grand job there."

Peering around the corner in the corridor, Sophie made sure that James was in his office, with the door closed.

He had a Do Not Disturb sign pinned on the door, handwritten in his near-illegible scrawl. He didn't look up when Sophie walked in without knocking, but she noticed the annoyed twitch of his top lip. He knew it was her, even with his head down, concentrating on the screen of his laptop. He feigned disinterest in the woman in front of him. His strategy was clear: to make a person feel so awkward in his presence they wanted to leave his office within seconds. Any charm from the early days long since departed.

Sophie cleared her voice. She didn't take her eyes off him.

"I need to speak to you as a matter of urgency, James."

"Nope. I'm busy. You'll have to wait. Come back later this afternoon. But I can't guarantee anything. Big list to work through. Lot on my plate."

James stared at his laptop screen, one hand on the desk, fidgeting with his car keys. He didn't look up at her.

"No James, that won't do. I need to speak to you now. Right. Now. Stop looking at your screen and pay close attention to what I'm about to say to you."

Sophie closed the door softly. She had no intention of turning it into a performance for the whole office.

"That sounds ominous. What's up? Everything okay?"

James' tone changed. A look of genuine concern replaced the irritated frown of a few seconds before.

Sophie took the seat closest to James, placing her mobile phone on his desk. She maintained eye contact with him. Her forceful interruption unsettled him. His car keys fell to the floor, and he made no attempt to pick them up.

"I've been wondering why Alex left the theatre so suddenly. And why he didn't say goodbye to any of us. I was baffled."

Sophie paused for a few seconds, gazing intently at James. He shifted in his chair, no longer slouching in it, paying attention to her every word and maintaining eye contact.

"I've worked closely with Alex for years. We were more than colleagues, we were friends.

So, when he quit, with no heads-up or word of explanation, no goodbye, no leaving party, not even an announcement by email, I was more than curious. And the next bit really stumped me. With the pick of all the exceptional people here, why did you suddenly fill his boots? You don't have the expertise, or the contacts, let alone the leadership skills crucial for the role. None of this made sense to me."

She paused again, formulating her words slowly and deliberately.

"Not. One. Bit."

"So, I decided to...well, rather than telling you what I decided to do, I want you to listen to this."

She pressed the play icon on her mobile phone, making sure the volume was turned up so he could hear every word.

"So have you thought any more about our conversation, Alex?"

"Yes, I have but surely, James, can we not come to a different arrangement?"

"No Alex, you know my terms. We've spoken about this before.

You resign, leave immediately and recommend me to the board as your replacement, or I tell your wife about the sordid little affair you've been having."

"But James, you know that affair's over now. Why are you doing this to me? I thought we were friends. I confided in you. I can't believe you're being so cruel. And this is surely blackmail?"

"Oh, please don't be so pathetic, Alex. You're deluded. We were never friends. It's time for you to choose. This place or your marriage. Up to you."

Sophie stopped the recording. James had obviously got the picture.

He stared at Sophie. The colour left his face, and his mouth twisted with rage.

"How the Hell did you get that?"

Sophie smiled. She didn't care. James could get as angry as he liked. The conversation was only going one way, and she was in control of it.

"Alex had the presence of mind to record some of your little chat. He recorded enough to incriminate you. It's a shame he never thought to copy the files on your computer before he left, but he knew about those sordid home-videos you watch. And now I do."

Sophie leaned forward; her eyes locked on James' eyes.

"The thing is James; I couldn't understand Alex just leaving without saying goodbye to any of us, so I decided to pay him a visit. To begin with, he stuck to your story of him resigning because of ill health and wanting to leave quietly to avoid discussing personal details. Eventually he told me the truth. How he'd let slip about his affair to you during one of the vape breaks and how you'd blackmailed him into resigning and recommending you for his job. I couldn't believe what he was telling me, so at that point he played the recording. I was horrified and dumbfounded. What a despicable creature you are, James."

The rage in James' eyes would have made a lesser person flinch and whilst Sophie felt a little uneasy, she continued speaking without looking away.

"You know he's lost everything, right? He told his wife about the affair, and she left him and took the kids. Their house is now up for sale. He's completely broken, James, and you did that to him. And why? Just to get his job, for crying out loud? You're pathetic, James. You don't deserve Alex's job and you're nothing compared to him.

The board may well have rubber stamped his recommendation and put you in charge, but the tables have turned now, haven't they James? It's your turn to face an ultimatum!"

"You've got nothing on me. That recording would be inadmissible in court and believe me, you'll need to go to court if you want me out. I'll not be blackmailed, I'm not scared of that recording, you're the pathetic one if you think you'll be sitting here."

Sophie nodded. James leaned back in his chair as though he'd won.

Sophie watched his smile of victory waver and fade as she didn't move from the chair.

"I see. You think that's all I have on you? You think perhaps you've covered your tracks, that your behaviour hasn't been watched, witnessed and recorded? That I'm the only one angry with what you've put Alex through? You seem to have forgotten Diana."

"I don't know anyone named Diana."

"That's true, you don't know her name. You never got around to finding out what it was, she only stayed the one day. In that one day, you terrified her when you cornered her in your office.

She didn't stick around, though, she ran right out of the theatre and never came back."

"You can't prove a thing."

Sophie locked his eyes with her glare. She pointed up at the corner of the room behind her, then at the opposite corner, to tiny digital cameras. One camera would have been enough, but with both, James knew his actions towards Diana had been caught, recorded and were in Sophie's possession. Blinded by his inflated ego and arrogance, the cameras had somehow slipped his mind when he was shouting at Diana.

Game over.

Sophie went on to explain that James was to resign from his role within the week or she would release the recordings to the board members and other theatre employees. The irony was not lost on her that she was now effectively blackmailing the blackmailer, but she felt that a sense of natural justice was on her side. She did not allow herself to feel guilty in any way.

As it turned out, she didn't have to wait long before realising her plan had worked. Within a few hours of confronting James, rumours began to circulate that he had handed in his notice citing 'unforeseen personal circumstances' as the reason for his sudden departure.

Relief washed over Sophie as she was driving home much later that evening. James' resignation had indeed been made, with no accompanying fuss or drama, thankfully. As planned, she also resigned shortly after. The office grapevine buzzed with yet more unexpected and surprising news. Sophie had no intention of explaining to anyone what had really happened to warrant the three resignations, just weeks apart. When the dust settled a little, she would share her new plans with the team, but for the moment, there had been more than enough antics for one day.

She doubted it would be the last time James tried to pull something so loathsome and insidious. People like James were adept at reinventing themselves and creating false personas. It was clear from their parting words that he felt no remorse for the way he behaved. He was simply angry that Sophie had found him out, caught him out, and got him out. He believed Alex deserved everything he got for having an affair. It was just bad luck that Sophie had been on his case.

James was convinced that when Sophie demanded his resignation, her ulterior motive was purely to get his job for herself.

She poured scorn over the theory and told him that it was not his job in the first place. The fact that he had got the job solely on his ability to blackmail Alex and that Sophie didn't want it under any circumstances, never occurred to him. By the end of their conversation, he was under no illusions and could see that Sophie was deadly serious in what she said to him. He knew she would be true to her word if he did not follow her instructions to the letter. He might have got away with blackmailing Alex, but Sophie was an altogether different person.

He had never met anyone like her.

She was tenacious, uncompromising, and quite scary. Calling her bluff would lead to more trouble than it was worth, he quickly realised.

Sophie thought about her next meeting with Alex, in the morning.

She was incredibly disappointed by his behaviour; not just in having an affair which was bad enough, but in his obvious lack of judgement where James was concerned. Alex had not seen what lurked behind James' enthusiasm to join him on his vape breaks. He had been naïve and gullible to such an extent that he trusted James enough to talk candidly about his past affair.

In his defence, people like James were skilful puppeteers, adept at hiding their true motives, and expert at playing people without them realising. Alex allowed himself to be lulled into a false sense of security by James appearing genuinely interested in his life.

It had indeed cost Alex everything. Whilst his wife, Saskia was appalled when Alex told her about the real reasons behind his sudden resignation, she could not bring herself to forgive him enough to save their marriage. It was a bridge too far. Their teenaged children felt the same.

As for Sophie, she was true to her word.

She did not want Alex's job, although the board would have offered it to her. Instead, she planned to work her four weeks' notice period as agreed. She would ensure all the loose ends of her projects were tied up, so her assistant, Maggy, was left in a position where she could easily step into her role.

For several months she had been training Maggy as an understudy for the role of PR manager. Sophie knew that with Maggy, she was leaving the theatre in safe and talented hands. Thankfully, the board agreed with Sophie, which made her resignation more palatable to them.

Later that evening, snuggled up in bed with her French Bulldog, Psmith, Sophie opened her laptop. It was time to put the finishing touches to her new business venture: Canine Companions and Dog Walking. It had been many months in the making. She reached the conclusion that corporate life was not for her, irrespective of the whole saga with James and Alex. She wanted a new challenge, where she took control of her own destiny, where her days were enjoyable and full of fresh air.

And Sophie really loved dogs.

They were uncomplicated, loyal, and lovable. And the best company ever! The thought of taking her favourite fur friends on long walks and being paid for the privilege was something she had been thinking about for a long time.

She was now just four weeks away from her dream becoming a reality.

჻

*Let me tell you the secret
that has led me to my goals:
my strength lies solely
in my tenacity.*

Louis Pasteur

Chapter 9

Kelly

W e're ready for you, Kelly!" The production assistant's cheery tone put an abrupt end to Kelly's breathing exercises. Within seconds, her heart began to pound again.

"She is looking gorgeous, Patricia."

The stylist, Evie, applied a final spritz of spray to Kelly's shimmering hair, freshly tamed of its tangles.

"The cameras are going to love her."

Staring at her reflection in the mirror, which she had avoided until that moment, Kelly could see that Evie had indeed worked wonders. Gone were any traces of last night's insomnia. And her makeup, although heavy for a daytime look, did make the most of her features. Evie reassured her that the combination of primer, foundation, tint, blusher, highlighter and fixing spray was what the cameras demanded. Any less and she would look washed-out.

"Thank you, I love my hair. How you've managed to get it looking so straight and sleek is beyond me. Can I take you home with me please?"

Evie nodded her head.

"Of course, provided you give me plenty of time off for clothes' shopping and a generous discount. Now, I hope you enjoy the interviews. Just be yourself."

Taking one last look in the mirror, this time at her outfit, a stunning patterned maxi-dress from her favourite designer, Kelly joined Patricia for what felt like the longest walk of her life, to the film studio.

Patricia tried to distract Kelly with small talk so the few minutes' walk would not be made in silence. She knew how nerves could get the better of even the most experienced and confident interviewees.

Silences were to be avoided.

"So, how are you feeling about today's interview, Kelly? I hope you're over the moon at the thought of becoming a reality tv star. We're all convinced this programme is going to fly."

"Oh gosh, I'm experiencing a mad rush of feelings...I think. Being given this space to promote my business and share my journey is exciting. But..."

Kelly's voice trailed off for a few moments as she became aware of her pounding heart, again.

"...I would be lying if I said I was chilled out. I've been flip-flopping between happy one minute and absolutely petrified the next. But right now, I'm calm; or at least, I'm telling myself I am. Everyone I've met is so friendly and encouraging, so I have no doubt that I'm in the best of hands. And Evie has given me the most stunning make-over ever, so what a start to the day!"

"We'll look after you Kelly. And nerves are natural, so try not to focus on them too much. The secret is not to let go of the butterflies in your tummy, but to let them fly in formation! And don't forget that everyone is rooting for you. Today is simply about creating content to promote the programme, with the aim of showing you in a natural light. We don't expect you to be a polished pro, and our viewers won't either. Besides, that would come across as disingenuous. Just be yourself, but the best version of you. Well, here we are."

Patricia opened the door to a large studio, and gently ushered Kelly in.

"As you know, you're being interviewed by Beth, who is an absolute professional and a great woman, too. She'll put you at ease. And I'll be back in 40 minutes to take you to your first magazine interview, two floors down, so we don't even have to leave the building. Good luck, Kelly. Enjoy the experience!"

"Thank you, Patricia. Your words are so kind, and your advice has been great. I just love that about butterflies. Oh no...apologies...my mobile is ringing. Please give me two ticks, I'll make it brief and turn it off straight after."

Kelly could see that Jake was calling and given they had spoken earlier, when she was in hair and make-up, it could be something serious. Best to answer, and best to make it quick.

"Hi Jake. I'm in the studio, about to be interviewed. Is everything ok?"

"Hi Kelly, absolutely nothing to worry about. Just two things. Ben Morris, the editor of AAH magazine has just rung. He wants to interview you for their February edition, but it must be next week. I've checked your diary, and you're free on Monday at 11am. I just need to confirm this with him urgently. I didn't want to guess and double book you, and I know we're filming on Thursday of next week. Secondly, I know that you're going to be on your game today.

Remember what we said about Imposter Syndrome? You've got to kick it to the kerb and bask in your light, girl! Stand in your power. And shine! You've earned this."

"Ahh, thank you, Jake. I'm feeling nervous but excited. Yes to the interview, and the time is perfect. I love their magazine, so we don't want to miss out. Please thank Ben on my behalf, too. It's all so very exciting!"

Out of the corner of her eye, Kelly could see Beth looking in her direction and gesturing that they were ready for her.

"I've got to go, Jake. I'll ring you when I'm on the train. Lots of love. Bye."

"I am so sorry for that. I've turned my mobile off now."

With an apologetic smile, Kelly sat down facing Beth.

And breathe...remember not to gabble and no umming and ahhing...don't panic. If in doubt, take a moment. I'm a strong and positive woman...I've earned the right to be here...I'm more than enough. Oh lord I feel sick...

Beth looked at Kelly, a smile on her face.

"Before I start the interview, Kelly, I want to reassure you that the production team will be taking your answers and using snippets of them for the pre-show promotional content. So don't worry if you start thinking midway through a sentence that your answer is taking too long, because this will not affect the promo videos and clips. However, if I do think that you're saying too much on something we've covered and no more needs to be said, I'll let you know by doing this."

She touched her fringe.

"The most important things are that you speak clearly, and don't rush your answers. Talking rapidly will affect your breathing, which will then make you feel nervous. It's the responsibility of the production team to decide what to include and what to leave on the cutting room floor. Try not to worry about anything. Just focus on answering my questions, using all your experience to guide you. You're in my capable hands, so sit back and enjoy our chat because that's all it really is!"

Something clicked inside her head, because Kelly beamed back at Beth and nodded her head in agreement. She felt much calmer, and everything Beth had said reassured her. It was not going to be a live, combative interview, in which Beth would be trying to catch her out.

It was just a conversation, answering questions and then allowing the production team to work their magic, afterwards. They wanted her to be natural. She could do that.

Just don't rush. Don't over think your answers…

"Thanks, Beth. I'm really looking forward to this. It's an absolute privilege to be interviewed by you. So, ready when you are!"

Showtime! Time to bask in her light and stand in her power, as Jake had so beautifully put it.

"Kelly, how did you start your business, and how did customers initially react?"

Beth wanted to put Kelly at ease, so it was a natural starting point.

Kelly liked the question. It was one she could answer spontaneously, without having to rack her brains for the answer.

"I started at a local market in my hometown. Initially, I was selling jumpers from a supplier in Italy. And I still use them today. I wanted to offer knitwear that wasn't available on the high street.

So, my jumpers had to be unusual but beautiful with a fashion twist. It could be that the sleeves or the hemlines were tipped with a contrasting colour, or the fabric was beautiful but unusual, giving the jumper that real luxe appeal. I wanted to create the concept of opulence minus the big price tag.

The reaction from customers was fantastic and many became repeat buyers. I added blouses and t-shirts, and then jackets, jeans, and accessories. Always with the same idea, to provide something with the emphasis on chic and effortless style at a reasonable price. I wanted my customers to be able to afford several pieces, buying an entire outfit, rather than just a standalone item."

Kelly paused to catch her breath and slow down a little. Beth did not give any sign that she was talking too much.

"Every week for three years, I was behind that market stall, until in the end, I had enough confidence and enough cash to rent a unit and have a proper shop front. Many of those original customers followed, and are still with me today, 15 years later. My philosophy now is exactly as it was when I started. I'm offering affordable luxury with clothes that are just that bit special and different to the high street."

Beth seemed pleased enough with Kelly's answer. One down and feeling good.

"You talk about your supplier from Italy, I would imagine it was hard to find suppliers in those early months of trading?"

Another good question from Beth. Kelly began to relax, no longer concentrating on her breathing.

"I found my suppliers through a few different channels. Trade shows was one avenue. Nothing beats visiting a huge room full of suppliers, seeing their clothes, and talking about their collections. I visited loads of those shows. It wasn't easy to find a great supplier that was not already supplying other businesses in and around my hometown, but somehow, I managed to pull it off.

I also used the internet, so I could investigate a supplier's back story, how they made the clothes, their ethics, and their customer service reviews. I would then have to haggle for the best credit terms and the best prices. That wasn't easy either. When you have little, or in my case, no trading history and you're a new business, most suppliers aren't willing to take a risk on you and offer you credit. I couldn't afford to order hundreds of items and pay cash up front, so I needed to be persuasive!

Eventually, one supplier, my Italian knitwear brand, took a calculated risk and offered me a small line of credit. It was enough to give me that early lucky break. Other suppliers then followed as my trading history developed, they could see that my orders were of a decent size, and I paid my invoices promptly.

I didn't tell them that I was operating from a market stall, even though it was by far the most glamorous stall at the market."

Kelly paused. Time to catch her breath and wait for the next question. She had reached her limit on that one.

"Every business needs a lucky break, Kelly, so that's good to hear. And now can we talk about your customers? Who buys from The Boutique? You say many are still with you from those early days."

The questions were getting better by the minute.

"I love that question!"

Kelly felt like jumping out of her chair and hugging Beth.

"I would say that my archetypal customer is a fashion-conscious woman who loves clothes. However, she doesn't want to be dictated to by flights of fashion.

She has her own mind, and she wants to feel good in what she wears, regardless of her size or shape. She trusts me, and my manager, Jake, to find clothes that, whilst they're inspired by the current catwalk trends, are also timeless and beautiful.

Some customers will buy one or two items of clothing occasionally, whereas others will fill their entire wardrobe with clothes from The Boutique. Many enjoy the feeling of community that we've created over the years. We don't just provide clothes and accessories and offer style advice; we're part of their lives. They talk to us, and share what's happening, the good and the not so good.

Lisa was my very first customer. She bought three jumpers which was a real boost at that time. She was, still is, a smart and sassy lady who loves her fashion. Chelle, Lisa's sister was my second customer. They both visited my stall together on that first day, but Lisa beat Chelle to the till! I remember that Chelle bought several jumpers, which was a huge vote of confidence. She's a real lover of fashion, and a stylish woman, not afraid to experiment and be daring with her choices."

Kelly noticed that Beth patted her fringe. She shot her another apologetic look.

Kelly could talk about her customers all day long. She was only just getting started, but clearly, according to Beth's fringe, it was time to stop.

"So, what keeps you awake at night, Kelly?"

"Gosh, that's…"

Kelly paused for a few seconds to gather her thoughts.

"I would say two things. One is sales slowing down, which is the biggest cause of insomnia with most small business owners, I think. If we don't meet our targets, for example, during the summer holidays, I'll lie awake at night worrying. Have I lost my buying skills? Have I misinterpreted styles and colours? Where have my customers gone?

These thoughts and more will fill my mind until the early hours.

I'm a worrier by nature, so I find myself leaning on Jake, to reassure me that my fears are not facts. It's just me living inside my head again. And this only happens for two weeks in the summer holidays, thankfully.

The other thing that keeps me awake, is when we experience a big rush on an item of clothing, and I've not ordered enough to cope with the demand.

Since we've been selling online, I've noticed a direct link between what the online fashion influencers are talking about, and the corresponding pieces that we sell. They may not be quite as edgy or dramatic as the item of clothing an influencer is highlighting, but if the clothes are similar, and if the customers are inspired by that trend, they'll sell out overnight."

Kelly glanced at Beth. She was fully engaged in her response. No fingers near fringes. Permission to continue. Kelly was on fire, she loved talking about her two favourite subjects, fashion, and customers.

How could she have been so nervous beforehand? She continued, on a roll.

"For example, a few weeks ago, I introduced a line of fine knit polo neck jumpers in cream, taupe, red, grey, and caramel shades. They had the most gorgeous and luxurious colour matching deep faux fur cuffs. Understated glamour at its finest! They sold out within hours, with many customers buying more than one. I traced this rush back to several fashion influencers on Instagram rating the faux fur trim as this year's must-have look for jumpers.

When something like this happens, I do lie awake at night, annoyed with myself that I didn't anticipate the demand from customers, because it's not always possible to go back and place another order. Thankfully, these situations are rare, and I did manage to order more of the furry cuffs, so I didn't spare the horses on the quantities that time! Over the years, I've been able to match my order sizes with the demand from customers fairly accurately, although it's not always possible.

But to answer your question in one sentence, not enough sales, and a mad rush on an item of clothing keeps me awake at night, for longer than I care to admit!"

Kelly looked at Beth who was nodding her head and smiling at her. All good!

"Faux fur cuffs? Sounds decadent. I'm missing out on this fashion trend!"

Kelly made a mental note to text Jake and ask him to put one of the jumpers aside for Beth as soon as the next order landed.

"My final question, Kelly. Would you describe yourself as a born entrepreneur?"

Kelly was relieved it was Beth's last question. Thankfully, she knew what to say, because she had been asked something similar in a previous interview with a journalist from a local newspaper. It felt more serious being asked it in a television studio, however. Her answer needed to be robust and considered.

"I'd say no, I'm not. There are other more brilliant business people you see, and it's clear why they're so successful. They have entrepreneur written all over them. That's not me. I think my love of fashion and the need to earn money as a single mum drove me in the early days, and it made me want to succeed."

Kelly paused. She did not want to say too much about her son, Teddy. She had agreed with him beforehand that he was off limits.

"I'm also quite stubborn by nature...I don't take no for an answer. I will always push myself to reach any goal I've set...I don't give up easily. And I will take calculated risks. For example, investing heavily in our online shop, and taking on a bigger unit. However, underlying everything, is my love for what I do. There's not a day goes by that I'm not grateful to my customers, to Jake and to my son. In their own different and unique ways, they've inspired me to reach my goals and accomplish something amazing. Well, it's amazing to me."

Kelly paused again, embarrassed when her voice became wobbly, and her eyes started to fill with tears.

Still no gesturing from Beth. She calmed herself. It was not the time for a takeover of tears.

"No, I'm not a natural born entrepreneur, Beth, just a woman who works hard, loves what she does, and is prepared to go on that road less travelled to make things happen."

"Okay. Cut. It's a wrap!"

The interview ended.

Beth leaned forward, taking Kelly's hands in hers.

"That was perfect, Kelly. I loved your answers. And you are so inspirational, so gutsy, and so endearing. And I would say, having interviewed many people over the years, that you are most definitely a natural born entrepreneur. There will be some great content that can be used from this interview, so pat yourself on the back. You did an excellent job. I understand that you are now heading for a few magazine interviews. If you can deliver anything like this, you'll be on the front covers!"

Beth stood up, removed her glasses, and patted down her jacket.

"It was lovely to meet you."

Patricia returned with some news for Kelly, which was happily received. Her next interview had been delayed by half an hour. She could enjoy a short break, and then it was back to Evie for hair and make-up retouches.

The first magazine interview was in stark contrast to Kelly's conversation with Beth. The journalist was interested in Kelly's fashion experience. Could she share her top style tips with their readers? What was in her wardrobe, and how often did she replenish it? Which clothes did she give to charity, and why? What were the upcoming fashion trends for the year ahead? How could their readers build a stylish capsule wardrobe on a small budget? What makes a woman stylish? What are the signs that suggest a woman needs a style makeover?

Kelly really enjoyed answering the questions. Her answers were authentic and thorough. The journalist was delighted with Kelly's openness and willingness to share as much as she could in the short time they had together. Kelly also offered to style three of their readers as a competition prize, and that went down very well.

The final interview of the day was the one Kelly found to be most challenging. She was mentally drained, and she didn't especially warm to the questions.

The journalist was writing a feature on women in business, so he was not especially interested in The Boutique. He focussed more on Kelly's approach to business. His 10 questions were rattled off in 30 minutes. Kelly realised, from her lacklustre responses to some of them, that she was at her best talking about The Boutique's customers and her love of styling and fashion, rather than sharing her business ideas and achievements.

She was, however, immensely grateful to the production team for arranging all the publicity. Undoubtedly it would help The Boutique, and drive more sales, something that was always close to her heart.

"Right, Kelly, before we let you go, I want to walk you through what's happening next week, when we start filming at The Boutique."

Patricia returned and took Kelly to the coffee lounge, both women grateful for an end of day sit down over a cup of coffee.

Kelly was finding it hard to concentrate. She worked long hours on her business, but this type of work was something altogether different. The need to focus on every word coming out of Patricia's mouth became more of an effort because of her weariness.

She gave herself a mental talking-to.

"Snap out of it! Now's not the time to allow my concentration to drift. I have the train journey home for that."

"The crew will be with you next Thursday at 9 am. As you know, from the earlier trial run, and the detailed filming schedule we've shared with you, it takes about two hours to set up, so you'll have to open an hour later than usual. We've talked about the importance of letting customers know what's happening a few days beforehand, so if you could send out a reminder email to your database, that would be great. Customers that are camera shy can then stay away for the three days we will be onsite, filming. We usually find that most people are happy to be filmed, especially when the camera is not being pointed at them specifically, but every customer that comes in will be asked briefly if they consent to being filmed. You have the form for that, and we will need to see any completed forms before you open the doors for business.

We will film Jake separately, for at least two face-to-face interviews, and I know from speaking to him earlier that he's already very well prepared for our agenda."

Kelly smiled, thinking of Jake. He would be more than happy to talk to the cameras and to be filmed in general.

He had already planned nine outfits with matching brooches and rings for the three days. If anyone was likely to be a natural with a lens pointed at them, it was Jake.

"Yes, everything is clear, Patricia, and you've been brilliant. Thank you for walking me through what's planned during the three days you're all with us. I don't think I have any concerns or questions at this stage. Oh, and I've read through the filming schedule several times. It was so helpful to have the breakdown of who's doing what and when, so there are no surprises there."

Kelly sipped at her perfect coffee. Nothing to do with the beans or the milk, it was just long overdue after a day of mineral water and smoothies. She savoured every caffeine-infused sip.

"Well, if you have any questions, or want to talk about any aspect of the filming, you have my number. I'll ring you on Tuesday, and again on Wednesday, just to check that everything is okay at your end. It's been great having you here today, Kelly. Everyone I've spoken to has said how impressive you are, and how you clearly know your stuff – fashion and business. So, let's see how this translates into column inches and pictures. I'm hopeful of some decent coverage, so fingers crossed!"

Kelly marvelled at Patricia. What a woman, so efficient and friendly with it.

"Thank you, Patricia. It's been an unbelievable day for me, on so many fronts, and the interviews really pushed me out of my comfort zone. I enjoyed them all, but especially my interview with Beth. She's quite something isn't she? I will never forget today, and I'm so grateful to you and the production team. Thank you again for this incredible opportunity...
...oh, and the butterflies. They did fly in formation. I took your advice, and it worked."

As soon as she was on the train, Kelly rang Jake, as promised, to tell him about the day in as much detail as she could muster. It was no easy feat, given she felt not only mentally, but physically exhausted and wanted nothing more than to fall asleep and be magically transported from the train to her bed, without waking up.

She still found it astonishing that all of this had arisen from one talk she gave at The Business Show in London. In the audience was a member of the production team. One conversation led to another, and now, just eight weeks later, she was on the edge of something truly extraordinary.

It all felt surreal.

It came at a time when she was looking to take The Boutique to the next stage. Kelly hadn't quite figured out what it entailed, but now the plan was playing out, and she was not having to do much more than hang on tight and join in.

She texted Jake to put aside one of the faux fur cuff jumpers for Beth. The soft grey one would really suit her. How awesome would it be if she saw Beth wearing it on the tv!

Her weary mind began to wander.

How were they going to manage all the new customers that would come their way after the programme aired? And what about the extra stock she would have to order? And their Instagram followers? They would surely reach 150,000. Jake would have to go into overdrive to create new content to feed the followers. The online shop...she would have to find another pair of hands to upload all the new stock and keep it updated.

What a wonderful position to be in.

She drifted off to sleep, dreaming about suppliers, jumpers with furry cuffs and the orders she would need to place in the next few months.

The End ?

Acknowledgements

If your book is to be a top-notch production then several people must join the merry creative throng.

I start my roll call of appreciation with thanks to my editor, Dawn. A successful author in her own right, Dawn 'tickled my copy' (her words not mine) and was an absolute joy to work with. She proved that the bond that exists between author and editor is indeed a precious one.

Next up, the super talented designer, Cathy Hayes, who designed the striking cover of The Boutique, never once complaining at my umpteenth revision.

A big bouquet goes to Chris Day, the founder of Filament Publishing. Chris has also published two of my previous books but, for The Boutique, I was determined to self-publish. Chris was always in the wings providing invaluable support, never once declining my late evening calls!

My heartfelt thanks must also go to Josh, who responded to my many updates on characters and plot twists with his customary enthusiasm.

Malcolm, my other half, well what can I say? His help and support for me never waned throughout this entire process. It never does.

Finally, I must thank you for buying my book. I hope you enjoy reading The Boutique as much as I enjoyed writing it. Do get in touch and tell me your favourite characters and story lines. I would also love to know if you worked out the plot twists!

Nine special quotes for nine special people

When the manuscript for The Boutique was finally being laid out, I found myself with a little spare time on my hands.

Bliss!

I decided to spend some of this precious time, coffee to hand, thinking about my nine characters, where I had taken them on their journey in The Boutique and what might be ahead as they move on in life, excepting Astrid, of course. But, fear not, she has a compelling story to tell of her early years in business; something for another day and hopefully, another book!

A friend asked me, how I would describe my relationship with these special people succinctly if asked by a curious stranger. That got me thinking! I would say that personalities aside, for every single one, I feel quite protective, possibly maternal. And I would want to embrace each one in a warm hug and talk to them at length.

Some, for example, Sophie and Jake, I have a keen sense they would be protecting me if I asked for help, and they would be providing wise counsel! But they all feel like close friends, even family. And I would most definitely want to hang out with all of them.

How would I describe them? Well, I could write nine chapters in answer to this question. But, I decided instead, to search for quotes that best summed up the essence of everyone, or that really painted their picture in a few brushstrokes. You will see that for some, we had space to use the quote I chose for them. But I didn't forget the others.

Because here they are in their entirety, all nine quotes. I can't tell you how long I spent on this lovely little task, but suffice to say, it was light outdoors when I began searching and by the time the ninth quote had made it into the book, I was typing in the dark!

I would love to know what you think about my choices, if you agree with them or, if you would have chosen something different altogether.

Jake

"If they don't like you for being yourself, be yourself even more."

Taylor Swift

Becky

"Our greatest glory is not
in never falling,
but in rising
every time we fall."

Confucius

Holly

"I can be changed by
what happens to me,
but I refuse to be
reduced by it."

Maya Angelou

Amy

"The future belongs to
those who believe
in the beauty
of their dreams."

Eleanour Roosevelt

Astrid

"In order to
be irreplaceable
one must always
be different."

Coco Chanel

Mary

"Take love when
it comes
and
rejoice."

Jodi Picoult

Caroline

"If there ever comes a day
where we can't be together,
keep me in your heart.
I'll stay there forever."

A.A. Milne,
Winnie the Pooh

Sophie

"The difference between try
and triumph
is just a little umph."

Unknown

Kelly

"Let me tell you the secret that
has led me to my goals:
my strength lies solely
in my tenacity."

Louis Pasteur

The Boutique